Wild Angel
by
Carolee Joy

authorlink press
www.authorlink.com

Published by Authorlink Press
An imprint of Authorlink!
(http://www.authorlink.com)
3720 Millswood Dr.
Irving, Texas 75062, USA

First published by Authorlink Press
An imprint of Authorlink!
First Printing, July 1999

Printed in the United States of America

ISBN 1-928704-04-2

Dedication

For Nan, my first writer friend and the closest to an angel anyone will meet this side of heaven. Your encouragement and enthusiasm are an inspiration.

With Special Thanks:

To Doris Booth, a talented lady who knows how to make good things happen, and to Authorlink's wonderful staff, especially Elaine Lanmon, a gifted writer and a dedicated friend who always finds time to help.

Author's Notes

This is a work of fiction. All the names, characters, organizations, and events portrayed in this book are either the product of the author's imagination or are used fictitiously for verisimilitude. Any other resemblance to any organization, event, or actual person, living or dead, is unintended and entirely coincidental.

Chapter One

She hadn't expected him to have such a big–gun.

Ellie Winfield hadn't recovered from the shock of the shoulder holster lying on the dresser when suddenly the cowboy was standing before her, wearing only white briefs, a black Stetson and a wicked grin. He laid a pocket watch on the dresser beside the vicious looking weapon and a money clip a half an inch thick with bills.

Ellie twisted her fingers together, totally at a loss as to what he wanted her to do. Should she talk dirty to him? A little strip tease? Or just undress and get it over with?

He stretched out on the double bed, his broad shoulders practically spanning the mattress. Everything about the man was big, from his muscular chest to hands that could swallow two of hers, to feet three times the length of her size fives. She didn't even want to think about the scary territory that lay between the hard, flat planes of his abdomen and the muscular thighs sprinkled with dark hair.

He tipped his hat back with a broad finger. "Your turn, darlin'."

He meant to just lie there and watch her remove her clothes?

Unfortunately, her urban cowboy seemed to have sobered up considerably since leaving the honky-tonk on the outskirts of Austin. Any hopes she'd had of him simply falling asleep so she could quietly slip out with the cash he'd promised disappeared with each heated glance he gave her.

Ellie swallowed a lump the size of a tumbleweed. What would he think when he realized her fingers were shaking so badly she couldn't even undo the hooks on her black satin sheath? She tried to assume a confident air. At least she was attracted to him, more so than to any man she'd ever met. "Perhaps if you'd tell me what you like ...."

His grin grew even wider. "Whatever you'd like."

What she'd like was to run from the room and never look back. But she had to go through with this, for Lauren's sake. The five hundred dollars he'd promised her would pay for the plane ticket to see the heart specialist her baby sister needed so urgently.

Biting back tears of humiliation, she reached around and fumbled with the fastening of her dress. The slippery fabric slid away beneath her trembling fingers, eluding her efforts.

Shaking his head, he crooked a finger and beckoned. "Shoulda told me you weren't in any better shape than I am. I would never have let you drive."

Glad he had misjudged her awkwardness, Ellie

sank to the edge of the bed and turned her back. The Jaguar had been fun. Whoever Joshua Bell was, he obviously had a great deal of money. He'd never miss the little bit of cash she needed so desperately.

She lifted her hair off her nape and twisted the thick strands to one side. Holding her breath she waited for the heaviness of his hand on her and was surprised by the gentleness in his touch as he undid the hook and eye, then slid the back zipper down.

An air-conditioned chill slid over her skin when he eased the filmy sleeves down her arms and parted the dress completely. He whispered reassurances against her skin, and Ellie shivered. From the cold, she told herself. Not because his lips felt like velvet. Certainly not because his tongue was making little wet circles on her back.

He slid the dress down, clasped her waist with his big hands and turned her to him. Her plunging, black demi-bra must have been a good idea, because his green eyes darkened appreciatively. He licked a finger and trailed it over her skin, just above the lace cups, leaving a trail of moisture that again made her shiver.

"Take it off."

"The dress?" Throat dry, she surrendered to the urge to cover herself and clutched the gauzy fabric to her breasts.

His eyes twinkled. "Everything."

"Everything," she repeated, hoping she'd misunderstood, knowing she hadn't.

"Right down to your skin."

She could do this. She had to. "Why don't you get us a cold drink?"

He took a long draught from the champagne bottle he'd carried from the bar and extended it towards her. "A man shouldn't have to drink alone when he's got a beautiful woman with him."

Ellie shook her head. "Ice-water is fine. And while you're doing that, I'll get, uh, comfortable. The ice machine is probably just down the hall." And if she couldn't make herself submit to him in the next few minutes, she could dart out the door and into the night and never see him again.

He shook his head and looked a little less amused. "Ice bucket is full. Glasses are on the bathroom counter. And I like to watch."

He would. Sighing, Ellie took the bottle from him, swallowed a mouthful of fizz and handed the bottle back before she rose and slid her dress down her hips. "You never told me what you're celebrating." She stepped out of the borrowed designer creation and draped it carefully over the chair next to the bed.

The anger in his eyes practically knocked her over. "The death of a dynasty. Turn around." His voice was husky and edged with an emotion she couldn't identify. "Slowly."

Self-conscious of the image she presented in her black lace bra, garters and black stockings, she turned her back to him.

Warnings screeched along her nerves a split second before his huge hands cupped her shoulders and pulled her alongside the bed. His hot mouth devoured the back of her neck. Ellie shuddered and closed her eyes even as a thousand thrills chased down her spine.

Distance. She needed to detach herself mentally from the scene before the really horrible stuff started.

She couldn't.

One iron-banded arm wrapped around her waist while his other hand snapped open the front catch on her bra, then cupped the full breasts that spilled from it. His fingers plied the sensitive nipples and sent a shard of desire deep into her womb.

NO!

She couldn't let herself feel anything but knew of no way to stop. Even worse, she didn't want to let go of the taut anticipation stirring inside.

He pressed against her buttocks, the hard length of him burning through cotton and satin. He rotated his hips against her. "All of it off, darlin'." His breath blew warm and moist against her ear.

He relaxed his hold and slid the bra straps down her shoulders, then tossed the scrap of lace onto the floor. "Your stockings."

Ellie turned to face him. "Then take your hat off."

Eyes narrowed, he looked down at her. A flicker of fear fluttered inside, her voice quavered, but she refused to budge. "You want the rest off, the hat goes too."

An instant later, the black Stetson sailed across the room and landed on a worn, plaid couch. Thick hair had hidden beneath the hat. He settled back against the pillows, stacking his hands behind his head. "Your turn."

Trying to keep her morbidly fascinated gaze off the bulge in his briefs, she unfastened the garters and slowly rolled the silky stockings down and off. She laid them over the dress.

He motioned to her black panties and garter belt. "Last but not least."

Swallowing the remainder of her pride, Ellie stepped out of the scraps of satin and set them with the rest of her clothes.

He patted the space beside him. Ellie reluctantly perched on the edge of the bed. His hands stroked down her arm, gently smoothed over her breasts. "You're sure you've done this before?"

"Certainly." If you counted the backseat close encounter she'd almost had with Jimmy MacFarlan back in college. She straightened her spine, more to keep from leaning further into his tantalizing touch than from any confidence she might have once had.

"Well, I haven't."

Whipping her startled gaze to his, she saw the faintest trace of chagrin in his. "Paid for it, that is. Suppose you show me why I should this time."

He certainly was arrogant, but with his looks, she

wasn't surprised. Mussed from the hat, a lock of dark hair tumbled over his forehead. Trying to ease her own excruciating sense of nakedness, Ellie reached up and tentatively brushed it back. Black lashes framed eyes as green as spring leaves. All sinewy muscle without so much as a pinch of fat, he was gorgeous. Remembering the way he'd held her as they danced, the teasing brush of his lips against hers made longing flutter in her stomach. He seemed like such a decent man, despite the strange circumstances of their encounter. Kind and tender, too, she could see it in his eyes. If only . . .

"Protection," she mumbled and darted away. How she'd hoped it wouldn't come to this, but now she was glad her older sister, Jenna, had insisted she be prepared. She grabbed her cosmetics bag and dumped the contents on the bed, scrabbling through lipsticks and eyebrow pencils to find the condoms. She held up a handful of foil packets. "Your choice."

"You're a regular walking pharmacy," he muttered, plucking the items from her hand and tossing them on the nightstand. "But we're not quite to that point yet."

"We're not?" Her breath came out in a rush as he tackled her around the waist and playfully dragged her down. His mouth covered hers, smothering further attempts at delaying the inevitable.

He tasted of wine and hot, dark need. Despite her attempt to remain aloof, his tongue coaxed hers into an erotic dance that made her clutch his shoulders and press against him. She wove her fingers through his hair, shocked that the little moan she heard had come from her own throat.

His mouth left hers, and she wanted to weep at the loss until his lips found one breast, then the other. Rolling the nipple on his tongue, he stroked, laved and applied just the right amount of pressure to make her ache for his touch.

He pulled away and closed his eyes, muttering under his breath. "I can go slower. Usually. Take my briefs off, darlin'. I'll make it up to you next time."

Next time? Hands shaking, she tugged on the elastic, easing his underwear down. She jerked her gaze away from the erection throbbing near her face as she pulled his briefs off. He was huge. If he thought he was going to . . . . Well, there was just no way.

He handed her a foil packet and lay on his back. "Do the honors, would you?"

She dropped the packet. Picked it up and dropped it again. He opened one eye and stared, then plucked the packet from her. "I meant tonight, not next week."

He sheathed himself, then rolled her beneath him. The hard hot tip of him prodded for entry. Ellie squeezed her eyes shut.

Soon. It would all be over soon. Then the trembling seizing her would stop. She would have done what she came for, she could take the money and leave.

Suddenly the invasion stopped. Fear and disappointment warred within her. What if he changed his mind? What would she do?

"You should have told me you weren't ready, darlin'." Hot breath scorched her breasts, her stomach, her . . . . Oh my God. What was he doing?

Ellie speared her fingers into his hair and arched up into him, helpless to stop the sensations overwhelming her as his mouth claimed her in an intimate kiss. "No, no, no."

"Easy, sugar. Easy." As seductive as a moonlit night, his voice wrapped around her. His lips and tongue coaxed her, blocking out her awareness of everything but him and the heat waves pulsing through her. Just when she thought she'd rocket off the face of the earth, Joshua moved up her body, lifted her buttocks and pushed inside. Barely.

Ellie bit her lip to hold in a cry of pain. Relax, relax, relax. This wasn't the way she'd planned to surrender her virginity, but she'd given up dreams of white lace and bridal gowns years ago. Besides she had to do this for Lauren. She'd exhausted all other options.

A look of confusion crossed Joshua's face. Desperate to hide her secret, Ellie moaned and dug her fingernails into his rear. "Come on, cowboy. Show me what you've got."

Reaching between their bodies, he caressed her as

he eased further inside and murmured little words of encouragement. Discomfort and thoughts of what might have been fled under his skillful hands. Then he was stroking her with his body and a fever began to build. She moved with him, raising her hips, meeting his increasing thrusts with her own spiraling tension.

This was not supposed to feel good. If he continued to draw this out, she didn't think she could stand it.

She didn't want it to end. She needed it to. With every sweet thrust, she lost a little bit more of herself.

His breath mingled with hers. A sweet, musky taste enveloped her as his tongue took hers with the same fervor with which he claimed her body. He moved faster, taking her with him.

Deeper, laying claim to her soul.

She rode the storm with him, struggling to find something she'd never known until pleasure burst through her in wave after wave of blinding light. Feeling bound to him in a way she never would have believed possible, she wrapped her arms around him and held on. An instant later, he groaned, pushed deep enough inside to touch her heart, then collapsed on top of her.

Little minx. Drowsy from the booze and sex, Joshua Bellinghausen shifted the sleeping woman closer, rubbed his cheek against her soft hair and drifted. Despite how he'd probably feel in the cold, sober light of day, at this moment, emptiness clawing at his soul, he knew she was worth every penny.

And then some, he realized as desire flared to life once again when she wriggled her curvy buttocks against his erection.

One more time. He needed to lose himself inside her sweet softness just once more. Maybe then he'd forget everything else he'd lost.

One more time. What could it hurt? She'd agreed to spend the night. He intended to enjoy every minute of it.

He slid his hand between her legs, stroking, testing. She murmured something, turned her head and started to shift to her back. Joshua pressed a kiss to the corner of her mouth. "Don't move, sugar. I want to feel you like this."

She pressed her derriere more firmly against him and sighed, a sleepy little sound of acquiescence.

He rocked against her, savoring the tease of her flesh against his.

It wasn't enough. He needed in. Now. He groped behind him on the nightstand and withdrew an empty packet. Then another. And another.

Damn. He really should . . . . Ellie moved back and forth against him, rubbing until he thought he'd explode. For a woman who had acted like she didn't quite know where to put a condom, she sure caught on fast.

One more time. What could it hurt?

Wedging his knee between hers, he positioned himself and eased inside. Sweet heaven, she was hot and tight as if she'd been created just for him, for this moment. She wiggled around him and whimpered when he withdrew partway, then sighed when he glided in deeper.

Just for a moment. Then he'd stop, see if he could find—He couldn't remember. Wanting to linger over each tantalizing stroke, but not being able to, he wrapped his arm around her waist and buried himself. Then did it again. And again. Ellie tightened around him and cried out. He ignited. Knowing he should withdraw, he couldn't, driven by a demon stronger than rational thought.

Pulling her tight, he spilled into her as the last tremors of her climax faded. Nothing in his life had ever felt so damn good.

One last time. What could it hurt?

Ellie woke, the weight of the slumbering man squeezing the breath from her. She shifted around, and the pressure eased as he rolled to his side. Gradually the events of the night drifted past the barrier of sleep. What was she doing? He was finally asleep and instead of leaving the way she'd planned, she now curled around him like a kitten.

And that dream. The pleasure still lingered,

doused only by the returning sense of shame. If he weren't snoring enough to wake everyone in the Lamplighter Inn, she'd be certain he'd been awake earlier and claimed her one time more than she'd counted.

If only her future held someone as enticing as Joshua. If only she could turn in his embrace, cuddle closer and share the dawn with him. Weak light spilled in through the cracks of the draperies.

Daylight. Jenna had been waiting for her for hours. What was she going to think?

Cautiously lifting the sheet, Ellie eased away and slid out of bed. Joshua continued to snore. Thank goodness he slept like the dead. When he finally fell asleep that is. She'd thought he'd never quit. If the man could make love like that when he was drunk, she was certain she didn't have the stamina to see him when he was sober.

She longed for a shower and glanced at Joshua. Making any noise at all was too risky. Pulling a crushed windbreaker suit from her tote bag, she quickly dressed. Crawling on the floor, she gathered up panties and high heels, then removed her clothes from the chair and stuffed them into the bag.

The money. Although she didn't like the way it made her feel, she'd be damned if she'd leave without the money he promised.

She was damned, anyway. What had she done, giving herself to someone she didn't even know?

Wistful, she fingered the pocket watch. It looked

something like the one her grandfather had carried. Her cowboy was obviously as sentimental as he was practical. She tentatively poked at the gun. He seemed like such a sweet guy, why did he carry a gun?

She reached for the money clip and hesitated. God, this felt like stealing. If he woke up now, he probably would shoot her, since she'd be breaking the promise he'd extracted from her to be there when he opened his eyes. As drunk as he'd been that wouldn't be soon. She couldn't stay.

Joshua stirred and groaned, his arm stretching out over the bare spot where she'd lain. She had to get out of here. Now.

There couldn't be as much money in the clip as she'd first thought. Just one huge wad of twenties. Probably the entire amount he'd promised her. Well, she'd earned it. Mostly.

She'd count it later and worry about it after that.

Snatching up her shoes, she hurried to the door and eased the chain back. The door lock snapped like a firecracker. Ellie jumped.

Joshua mumbled something. In a complete panic, not daring to take a last look at him, she hurried out the door and shut it as quietly as possible.

Jenna was in their ancient pickup truck at the far end of the parking lot, slumped over the wheel. Barefoot, Ellie ran to the car and rapped on the window.

Jenna screamed, then blinked and reached across

the passenger seat to unlock the door. "Ellie. What in the world happened? I almost called the police."

"That would have been real helpful." Ellie scrambled inside and buckled her seat belt. "You're so dramatic. Must be the artist in you. Let's get of here."

Jenna started the car and pulled out onto the service road of the freeway. "You weren't supposed to stay all night," she fussed at Ellie, her tone and expression an accusation. "I was worried."

Ellie spread her hands. "I'm sorry, okay? As much as he drank at the bar, I thought he'd pass out before we got to the motel." She pulled down the visor and inspected herself. Hair tangled, circles under her eyes, third-degree whisker burn on her chin. She looked like a pass-around circus groupie.

What had she done? The enormity of her loss, the waste of what she should have shared with a husband she could never have, slammed into her like a runaway truck. She dug her hands into her eyes, but it was no use. Tears spilled out until she wept deep wrenching sobs that ripped from her heart.

Jenna pulled over to the side of the road and stopped. Wrapping her arms around her younger sister, she patted her hair, murmuring soothing words and silly platitudes until she started crying, too. "Oh, Ellie. I'm so sorry. You shouldn't have had to do that. I should have quit this ceramics stuff and gotten a real job. We should have sold that stupid bull when we had a chance. We should–"

Ellie hugged her hard, then eased away. "Enough. If only won't change a thing now." She flourished the money clip. "Let's hope this will be enough to get Lauren to that specialist. Then we'll go back to taking it one day at a time like we have for the past ten years." She pulled the bills from the clip. Two twenty-dollar bills concealed what was a stack of hundreds.

"Oh my God." Jenna's eyes grew round as saucers. "What did you have to do?"

Ellie swatted her arm. "Nothing unusual. At least I don't think so. He was sleeping, so I just took the whole thing." She hefted it in her palm. "I didn't think there'd be so much. What do we do now?"

Jenna put the truck in gear and pulled out onto the highway leading to the Texas Hill Country and home. "Run like hell and hope he never finds you."

Chapter Two

Something rumbled nearby. Joshua groaned and pulled the pillow over his aching head. One hand groped the space beside him and came up empty. He raised up and looked around the shabby room. Hey. She'd promised . . . . What? Where'd she go?

The pounding grew louder. Muffled shouts came from the door. Maybe she'd gone for coffee. He could use a keg or two. Hot, strong and black. Grabbing the sheet and wrapping it around his waist, Joshua rolled off the bed, padded to the door, then flung it open.

Backlit by the midday sun, his younger brother, Barrett, grinned and handed him an industrial size Styrofoam cup. "Well, well. The prodigal son. Thought you could use an eye opener. Or did you already have one?" Barrett winked and pushed past him into the room. Looking surprised to find Joshua alone, he flung himself on the cheap couch.

"I'd watch that smirk, Barrett. If your face freezes that way, you'll never catch a woman and have an heir." The aroma of strong coffee assaulted Joshua's senses. He shut the door and settled into a battered easy chair, ignoring the tufts of stuffing protruding from the cushions. Taking a deep gulp, he grimaced at the noxious brew. "You just change the oil in your car or what?"

"There's gratitude for you. I rouse myself at the crack of noon just to bring you coffee and make sure you didn't bang your brains out and all you can give me are insults."

"So who said I was even with someone?"

"Years of observation. Whenever you get that mad you do one of two things. Sometimes both." With exaggerated motions, he sniffed the air and exhaled dramatically. "My intuition tells me last night you did both."

Joshua scowled. "How did you find me?"

Barrett looked smug. "Just looked for the sleaziest motel near the wildest bar in Austin with a black Jaguar conspicuously parked nearby. So where is she?"

Joshua shrugged, hoping to convince himself and his nosy brother it didn't matter.

"More to the point—who is she?"

"I told you, what makes you so certain there was someone else here?"

"That might explain the empty champagne bottle." Barrett scratched his head. "And you could have changed your aftershave to something that smells like a combination of gardenias and sex. But if you weren't with someone, then I don't want to hear your explanation for the black lace bra lying on the floor."

Ignoring the stab of pain in his head, Joshua

jumped up and surveyed the room. Except for the bra, all of her stuff was gone. He strode to the dresser. So was his money clip.

What a damn fool he was. He'd been rolled. By some itty-bitty woman with incredible breasts and the face of an angel.

Following him, Barrett poked a finger at the remains of the foil wrappers. "Only five? You must have been really drunk."

"Six," he muttered automatically. Why he could remember the exact number of times he'd taken sanctuary in her sweet warmth, he wasn't sure, when he remembered little else. Like her name. What the hell was it? Hailey, Aileen, Elaine. Allie?

"Well, unless you're hiding something in your pocket," Barrett interrupted, giving him a significant once over with his gaze, "you'd better hope to hell it was only five times."

Joshua motioned impatiently at him. "Stuff the lectures. My money clip is gone."

Barrett straightened. "Holy shit. Granddad's money clip? Not to mention that wad of cash you were toting for who knows what reason. Check your jeans." He got on his knees and peered under the dresser, then beneath the bed. "Nope. Nothing but a few dust bunnies."

Anger building to a thunderous rage, Joshua patted the pockets of his black denims. Gone. He'd promised her five hundred dollars, and she'd taken the whole goddamned money clip.

What a chump he was.

Leaving Barrett sitting in the chair shaking his head and muttering about arrested development, Joshua stalked into the bathroom and slammed the door. A hot shower relieved the headache and the twinges in muscles recently tested, but although the water and strong soap washed her scent from his skin, he couldn't seem to get the faint whiff of flowers out of his nostrils. Nor wash the memory of her voluptuous little body out of his mind. She might have been tiny, but she definitely had a figure that would make a man's testosterone sit up and take notice. The sex had been better than fantastic. He'd never before been with a woman who'd made him feel as if he held the keys to the kingdom.

How could she have deceived him?

Wearing only his jeans, he stomped back into the bedroom, clutching the sheet in his fists. If he found—correction, when he found that woman, there'd be hell to pay. He stood in the center of the room, trying to ignore the headache radiating out from the base of his skull.

Barrett sat in a tattered chair by the window, long legs stretched out before him. "So how'd you like the funeral?"

"About like I always do. Just a good reason to get stinking drunk. Especially with the added bonus of hearing that freaking will." He wadded up the sheet and tossed it onto the bed.

"Like he was supposed to know he was going to

die before either one of us produced offspring?"

Resentment made the coffee burn up into his throat. "Well, it doesn't make sense to leave a fortune to children who don't exist yet with the proviso that until they appear, the reckless exes get to sit on a Board of Trustees overseeing it all? As trustees? What do you suppose he was thinking of?"

"It's called estate tax planning," Barrett pointed out. "He was just trying to minimize Uncle Sam's portion of what he'd slaved all his life for."

Not that their father didn't have the right to leave the ranch and dairy to anyone he chose, but with him and Barrett breaking their backs in the family business, it was a pretty low blow.

"Besides," Barrett continued. "It's just the principal. You and I control the income from the property."

"There won't be any income to worry about after that flock of loonies runs everything into the ground."

"He was setting things up for years down the road." Barrett rubbed a hand over his face. "For crying out loud, Joshua, the man didn't wake up last week and decide it would be a good day for an aneurysm. You think you're the only one hurting here?"

He placed his hand on Barrett's shoulder. "Sorry. It's just . . ."

"If it bugs you so much to see them get anything, then get busy and make some lady a little mama."

"Why don't you? I'm not sure it's worth it. It just royally ticks me off." Standing in front of the cloudy mirror, he ran a comb through his hair. He'd seen enough of marriage watching his father's constant parade of brides. After their mother died when Joshua was fifteen, and Barrett thirteen, Dad had gone through five more wives in the ensuing twenty years. Unfortunately, or fortunately, considering the ladies involved, none of the marriages "took".

"I thought Belinda did a nice job arranging everything."

Joshua pulled on his rumpled western shirt. "Well, why not? She practically lives at that crazy church. I don't know why Dad married her."

Barrett shrugged. "Why'd he marry any of them? Guess he didn't realize he could have screwed them without a license. Didn't you ever tell him?"

"Put a cork in it, would you?" Joshua flipped the bedspread back, with the remote hope that the money clip had gotten lost beneath the bedcovers. A gold compact fell to the floor. He picked it up and examined it. EW was engraved on it in elegant script. Okay, so it wasn't Allie. Then it must have been . . .

Barrett came over and stood beside him. He picked up the sheet Joshua had used as a toga and held it by the corner. "Holy moley. How old was this sweet young thing, big brother?"

Glancing down he followed Barrett's too-seeing

gaze to the white sheets and the unmistakable traces of blood. What the hell?

"You sure she was over the age of consent?"

"Yeah, she just wasn't old enough to be my mother, unlike the women you usually date," he retorted automatically while he mentally replayed as much of the night as he could remember. Her uncertainty, the awkwardness, the way she'd kind of scrunched her eyes shut the first time. "Come on cowboy. Show me what you've got." Damn, she'd been tight. And he was an idiot.

The room rang with Barrett's hoots of laughter. "I don't believe it. My brother, the legendary hit and run lover, got run over himself. By a virgin." Tears formed in his eyes as he clutched his side.

"She was a hook—" he broke off. It would be a big mistake to tell his brother just why he'd felt the need to pay a woman for the pleasure of her company. He never had before. What was it about her that had made him feel as if he'd been punched in the solar plexus?

Something about her sitting at the bar at that dumpy country-western joint. The way her dress had curled around her when she danced. The soft brush of her lips against his when he'd stolen a kiss. The tiny bit of hope flaring in her eyes when he'd pulled out his money clip and bought her a drink.

She'd looked so damn out of place. Every ridiculous protective instinct he possessed had overridden his common sense when a beefy trucker had started putting the moves on her. The guy's hand on her arm, and her look of absolute terror, had just about put him into a red rage. Hell, he'd had to get her out of there before he busted the place up.

Boy, had she set him up, but good.

Fuming, Joshua glanced from his brother to the evidence staining the white cotton sheets. Before there were liberated ladies with meters on their biological clocks, a man could feel safe from being used. Not any more.

Whatever the hell little Miss Innocent's game was he intended to find out. No matter what he had to do.

Arriving at the ranch did little to improve Joshua's mood. Usually the sight of the white columns, the tall trees surrounding the limestone two-story house filled him with a satisfied sense of homecoming. Not today. No sooner had he set foot on the wide porch than he and Barrett were accosted by a flock of concerned, cackling women. The exes.

"Where did you find him? Oh, the poor dear." Rosemary, replacement wife number one attacked in full mother armor. "Cook has lunch waiting, but if you'd like more of a brunch, maybe some eggs and ham. I'll whip it up while you clean up."

"You look like a tomcat home from the prowl." Esther, number two, pursed bright red lips, almost as if she expected him to share the details with her.

"It's a given he wasn't at the gym. Maybe a nice carrot tonic will perk you up." Gretchen, number five, a study in lemony-yellow spandex, scurried off right on Rosemary's heels, trying to beat her into the kitchen.

"Those clothes, darling." Monica wrinkled her nose, as if he actually stunk although he knew he didn't. "They look like you slept in them. A hot shower and a shave and you'll feel ever so much better."

Joshua rubbed a hand over his stubbled chin, his mood growing blacker by the moment.

"My money says he slept out of them." Esther cackled.

"I hope you haven't done anything to upset your inner peace." Belinda frowned. "Your aura is quite gray."

He was surprised it wasn't red, since that was the color of everything he looked at. "What are they doing here?" he muttered in an aside to Barrett.

"You invited them to stay as long as they wanted."

Now he knew he'd been crazy with anger. No wonder he'd gotten too tanked to make it back home. He knew what was waiting for him. Five well-meaning, but misguided stepmothers.

He held up his hands to ward off their good intentions. "Mothers, I appreciate your concern, and I apologize for making you worry, but I'm fine.

Please don't fuss, just carry on. I'm going to my
study to make some calls."

If anyone could get him some answers, his friend
DJ could. Joshua had spent ten years on the police
force before realizing several years ago that he
wanted to participate in the family business. DJ
Justice had also left the police force shortly
thereafter to launch a lucrative private investigation
business, but the two men had maintained the
friendship started under the closeness of danger.
The only remnants from Joshua's police days were
the Beretta he carried and the wad of cash he liked
to have to remind him that life held more than a
hazardous job busting drunks and fighting
bureaucrats.

Joshua called his friend the minute he closed the
door to the study. Unfortunately, Barrett opened the
door and came in without an invitation. Even worse,
he refused to take Joshua's blatant suggestion he
find somewhere else to park his can. Despite
Joshua's repeated attempts to get Barrett to leave
the room, his brother insisted on taking a ringside
seat, then sat there grinning like someone had
pushed the pause button on Ronald MacDonald.

DJ answered the phone on the third ring and
immediately recognized Joshua's voice. "Hey,
what's up?"

Joshua got right to the point. "I need you to find a
woman for me."

DJ chuckled. "Yeah, I heard about the will, but I

gotta tell you, I don't run a dating service here."

"Yeah, you fill in at the Comedy Club in your spare time." Joshua ran a hand through his hair. "I met this lady. I need you to do a background check, find out everything you can."

"What's her name?"

"I don't know."

"Where does she live? Work?"

Joshua exhaled noisily. "I don't know."

The sound of DJ's annoying habit of tapping a pen on the desk drifted over the line. "Okay, suppose you tell me what you do know."

"She's blonde. Really short, probably not even five-feet. Maybe weighs a hundred pounds, but most of it, I mean, she's built."

Barrett guffawed and continued to grin. Joshua glared at him.

"I met her at Dandy Don's Danceland. She was wearing a black, gauzy kind of thing."

"Okay, so I just go over there and ask everybody if they saw a blonde in a negligee."

"A dress." He visualized her shapely legs. "Really short. The dress. Made out of shiny, filmy stuff." He hefted the gold compact in his palm. "Her initials are EW "

"Well, at last. Something that might actually help." DJ sighed. "It's nothing to go on. Any idea how many blondes there are in Austin? Not to mention in the surrounding towns?"

"No, tell me." Exasperated with himself, and

getting madder by the moment at the woman, whoever the hell she was, Joshua slammed his fist on the desk. "Just find her. Call me as soon as you have anything."

"You know I'll do the best I can. But, don't expect miracles."

Joshua hung up the phone and met Barrett's goofy grin.

"Let me call you sweetheart. I can't remember your name," he sang.

"Oh, shut up."

"Really knocked you on your can didn't she?"

Joshua scowled. "I'm not going to let her get away with taking advantage of me."

"Poor little you." Barrett laughed. "You don't stand a chance of finding her."

"I will."

"Bet?"

Despite his better judgement and the sinking feeling he had that his brother might be right, Joshua refused to abandon the idea of seeing the woman again. She owed him, damn it. The money, the gold clip and . . . . For a moment, an image of her curled against him flashed through his mind, heating his blood. He forced the provocative picture and feelings away.

Hell, she just owed him. "Yeah. Double the amount she took from me. Not counting the value of Granddad's gold clip."

Barrett hesitated a moment, then chuckled and

slapped his palm. "Man, you're easy. You're on."

A week passed, then another. DJ called, but reported that although he'd found several people who remembered seeing the woman, no one knew who she was. They all remembered Joshua more.

Frustrated, Joshua began to think he'd not only be out the two thousand she had taken, but another four to Barrett. Which just proved one thing.

It was way past time he settled down and dealt with the terms of Dad's will. Either find a way to work through it, live at the ranch with the reckless exes, or find a woman he could marry on mutually agreeable terms which didn't include anything as idiotic as love. He'd spent too many years watching his father's grand passions fizzle into property settlements and alimony.

His thoughts turned relentlessly to EW, as he now preferred to think of her. Not being able to recall exactly what her first name was galled him to no end, but only for a moment. Then he was remembering the warm, sweet feel of her skin, the cloud of blonde hair, the dynamite in one tiny package.

Which proved another thing. When it came to women, there apparently was no limit to the idiocy a Bellinghausen would go through. He clenched his hands. He refused to be like his father, ruled by emotions rather than reason.

Pushing away thoughts of everything else except the production reports spread across his desk, he

shook his head and returned his attention to work.
But his gaze kept straying to the elegant and
obviously expensive gold compact on the edge of
the desk blotter. Another contradictory piece to the
puzzle.

Who was she?

All the questions only strengthened his resolve to
find her. Never mind that DJ, one of the best
investigators in the state, had failed to come up with
a lead. Joshua had a much more compelling reason
to locate her than mere money.

He hated riddles. Not knowing why she'd traded
her virtue to him for cash was driving him crazy.

Almost as much as the desire to see her again.

Chapter Three

The after effects of her wild night had long subsided, but two weeks later that wasn't what troubled Ellie. At thirty-two years of age, having grown up on a farm, she had learned to live with occasional physical discomfort. The lingering sense of shame and regret over her behavior were another matter. If it weren't for Lauren, she couldn't have done it. She wouldn't have. Her baby sister was worth anything, however. Ellie just wished she could push the incident from her mind.

Thinking of Joshua merely as an "incident" proved impossible. He'd become too indelibly etched on her mind, in her senses.

Ten-year-old Lauren, long blonde hair in pigtails, crept into the study where Ellie graded tests for her high school biology class. She hovered over Ellie's shoulder.

"That one's wrong." Childish pride filled Lauren's voice as she pointed with a slender finger. "I know more than those big kids. Why won't you let me go to school?"

Ellie sighed. They'd been over this territory a hundred times. Although her heart ached for her little sister, the risk of sending Lauren out among

other children was too great. "You know the answer
to that one, too, Buttercup."

Lauren flopped into a wingback chair. "It's not
fair. Other kids get to go to school, ride horses, have
roller-blades. Have fun. All I do is read, listen to
music, and play on my dumb computer. Borrring."

Her heart wrenching, Ellie continued working and
tried to act as if today were no different than any
other Saturday. "Lots of kids would like to go to
school at home."

Lauren scrunched up her face. "I'd rather be
dead."

Ellie's blood ran cold. She knew her sister didn't
mean it, that it was just childish anger, but it was so
close to the truth, she couldn't bear to hear the
words. If Lauren couldn't have another surgery,
soon, they would lose her.

Ellie would have only Jenna and no hope of ever
having children of her own because of the awful
reality of her own tainted genes. No hope for a
husband, either. What man didn't want a family of
his own? She wouldn't want the type of man who
didn't.

Jenna, dressed for travel in dark slacks and a
plum sweater, a lightweight jacket over her arm,
appeared in the doorway. "Lauren, do you have
your books packed? We need to leave."

"I don't want to go to Cleveland," Lauren
grumbled but rose to comply with her eldest sister.
"I don't want to have more doctors poking at me

like I'm some kind of freak!"

Ellie went to Lauren and put her arms around her. "I know this is awful, sweetie. But we've got to keep trying until we find someone who can help you. Get your coat. It's still winter there."

When Lauren left, Ellie turned to Jenna. "Sure you're going to be okay, just the two of you? I could probably take a leave of absence."

Jenna shook her head. "You're going to need it later, if they decide she's a good candidate for that surgery. Much as I hate to go without you, someone needs to stay here and mind the farm. We can't afford for you to risk losing your job, either." She embraced Ellie. "Thank you for what you did. I know what it cost you."

Ellie blinked back sudden tears and returned the hug. Jenna couldn't have a real clue as to how much Ellie's night with Joshua had shattered her peace of mind, but she couldn't let her older sister see how upset she still was over the whole thing.

Ellie was expected to be the strong one, a role she had assumed long before their mother's unexpected death ten years ago. Jenna had always been too sensitive, too much a worrier, forcing her younger sister to take charge in a crisis. When her sister released her, Ellie had regained control. "I didn't do anything you wouldn't have."

Jenna raised a brow. "Oh, yes you did. And it was a true sacrifice done in love for our precious baby sister." She squeezed Ellie's arm. "I'll never forget it, I promise not to mention it again. Providing you go for a check-up like I suggested."

"Yes, 'Mother'." In her gentle way, Jenna could be as tenacious as a pit bull. "I've got an appointment with Taylor next week in Austin, much as I hate to keep taking advantage of our friendship."

"She doesn't mind." Jenna turned at the door. "By the way, I got another call from the Bellinghausens about that bull. Don't be surprised if they show up."

"I thought Mr Bellinghausen died last month."

"He did. But his son insists on discussing the matter again."

Ellie made an exasperated noise. "Don't those people understand the word *no*?"

"Apparently not." Jenna shrugged. "I know you think we should try to build up the breeding business again, but are you sure we shouldn't just sell the beast? You're carrying a double load, your teaching job and the breeding. There's got to be an easier way to make this farm work."

Ellie sighed at the too-familiar argument. "The only way we can provide for the future is to make Ellison's Farm what it was. Only better. We can't do that if we don't have our prize bull."

"Then I leave the Bellinghausens in your capable hands."

"I can't wait." Ellie followed Jenna and Lauren out the door. She helped load the last of their bags into their neighbor's car for the drive to Houston where they'd catch a flight to Cleveland.

Danny Hirsch paused and grinned at her. "Don't worry about a thing, Ellie. I'll see them safely to the plane. And you be sure to call if I can help around here."

She wondered what they would have done the past few years without his quiet presence. Ten years older than Jenna, he acted more like a big brother than a friend. Sometimes Ellie wondered if he wasn't a little bit sweet on her older sister. Just about the time she would decide he was, she would realize he treated them all with equal consideration. Well, maybe he was a bit fonder of little Lauren, but they all were. She was a charmer, despite her ill health.

Returning to the porch, Ellie stood there and waved until the car disappeared around the curve in the lane. She sighed. With Lauren's constant need for attention and Jenna's frequent distracted air, Ellie usually had plenty to keep her mind occupied when memories of the cowboy haunted her. The next two weeks were going to be tough. Fortunately, she'd have plenty to keep her days busy. But the nights were going to be hell.

Spring scents wafted through the open window of Barrett's Chevy truck as the vehicle wound through the hills of central Texas. They'd already visited half a dozen small farms in Barrett's never ending quest for the perfect stud bull. Joshua watched the rolling hills go by and recalled that he'd decided to accompany his brother to relieve the tedium of a Sunday afternoon.

He'd realized two hours into the day he'd made a mistake, but Barrett seemed to be in high spirits. Probably thinking about how he was going to spend the money he'd conned Joshua into betting. Why had he agreed to that stupid bet? He was never going to find her.

Joshua rested his arm on the door and tried to remember the color of the woman's eyes. Blue, but not the bluish-purple of the bluebonnets clustered along the highway. More blue-green, like the rare stone in Mother's birthstone ring. No, the woman's eyes were more like . . .

Barrett turned onto a winding lane. A large sign proclaimed it as the way to Ellison's Farm. Home of Spotty, the world-renowned Jersey bull. The name of the farm hit Joshua between the eyes.

Why hadn't he remembered it sooner? "Ellie."

Barrett glanced away from the gravel road and frowned. "It's okay. You can call me Barrett."

"Not you, you idiot. I finally remembered her name. It's Ellie."

Barrett guffawed. "Only took you two weeks. How about a last name?"

Joshua drummed his fingers on the open window frame. "Not yet, but it's just a matter of time." Although he wasn't sure he could remember something he was certain he'd never known. It started with the W, though. Unless she'd pinched the gold compact.

Ellie. He rolled the name on his tongue. Sweet. The way she tasted.

Barrett relaxed his hands on the wheel. "I almost thought I saw four grand floating out of my pockets. What a relief. You'll never find her, Joshua."

Joshua refused to share his uncertainty with his brother. The possibility of Barrett being right increased the more time passed, but still…. She tugged at his thoughts constantly.

Because he didn't like being taken advantage of, that's all. She'd made a promise and broken it. She'd slipped out, a thief in the night, with four times the money he'd promised her, and the heirloom money clip that had belonged to his father's father.

The more he thought about it, the madder he got. No, the only reason he wanted to find Miss Not-so-innocent was to set the score straight. That was all. And to find out why she'd done it. Hadn't their night of loving meant anything to her? Did she awaken in the middle of the night yearning for his warmth beside her? The touch of his hand on her skin? He pushed the questions from his mind.

"Have you met this Ellison woman before? What was her name again?"

"Jenna. A real artsy-craftsy type. She makes clay pots and junk. I tagged along with Dad last time.

Beats me why she won't part with that bull. I
suspect it's because her sister has some grandiose
notion of building up the breeding stock."

"And she is?" Joshua asked, more for the sake of
gathering information that might later prove useful
than for any real interest.

"Don't know. Teaches biology at the high school.
Probably fancies herself as an expert on animal
husbandry."

Joshua immediately visualized a pale, flat-
chested, middle-aged spinster, glasses resting on the
end of a pinched nose. "I get the picture."

The winding lane ended in front of an old,
limestone house that looked lovingly cared for
despite the fact that the wood trim and porch
probably hadn't seen a fresh coat of paint in years.
Massed beds of pink and white petunias clustered
around the walkway leading to the porch where
white wicker furniture sat, inviting visitors to sit a
spell. Beyond the house, a carpet of sunflowers and
pink primroses spread to the limestone banks of the
blue-green water of the Blanco River.

Barrett rapped on the door. Wind chimes clinked,
but otherwise the house was silent.

Immersed in her calculations, Ellie heard Ginger,
Lauren's sheltie, bark but ignored her. If she paid
off half the feed bill and the truck insurance, maybe
she could rent the south pasture to Danny again this

summer and stretch the cowboy's money just a little
bit further. That just might work.

The rapping grew louder along with Ginger's
frantic yipping. She pulled herself into the present.
Two-thirty. She'd gone to work as soon as she'd
returned from church and had lost track of the time.

She rose and made her way to the foyer. Two tall
men dressed in jeans and western shirts stood on the
porch, cowboy hats shading their faces. Jenna had
said one of the Bellinghausens might show up, but
she hadn't said the son would have someone with
him. Maybe it was his ranch foreman.

Tucking a loose strand into her neat French braid,
Ellie opened the door. Her heart froze as she
recognized the man gazing out over the side yard.
Oh, my God. Her cowboy. What was he doing here?
How had he found her? What was she going to do
now? Why, oh why, hadn't she checked to see who
was there before flinging the door open?

Maybe this wasn't Mr Bellinghausen at all, but
Joshua and a sheriff's deputy about to serve her with
a warrant. Pulse pounding, palms sweating, she
stepped back into the shadows of the hall. He'd
been so drunk. Maybe he wouldn't recognize her
with her clothes on. "Can I help you?" Please, let it
all be a mistake, she prayed. What was she going to
do?

Joshua stood half a step behind Barrett. That voice. Like something out of a midnight dream. His breathing temporarily stopped, as if he'd been thrown from a horse. He looked again, certain he'd erred. It was *her*.

Heart pounding, he couldn't help but stare, remembering her in black lace and an innocently wicked smile. He took in her demure clothes, the conservative hairstyle. Sure she looked different, not just because she wasn't half naked. Her hair and the style of her dress nearly made him think he was making a mistake.

Almost, but not quite. In flat-heeled shoes, she looked even shorter. And vulnerable, again arousing his protective instincts. Damn.

What was it that made him want to sweep her into his arms and take care of her?

He continued to stare. The long, loose jumper came practically to her ankles. A pale yellow blouse sprinkled with blue flowers brought out the blue-green of her eyes, and set off golden hair pulled severely from her face in some kind of braid. A yellow bow clung to the back of her head. She looked like she should be leading a kindergarten class, not turning tricks.

Barrett extended a hand. "Please, ma'am, I'm Barrett Bellinghausen. And this is–" His breath came out in a whoosh as Joshua stepped forward, his elbow connecting with Barrett's mid-section. He didn't offer his hand, afraid to risk exposing his feelings by touching her in front of his brother.

"Ranch foreman, ma'am. Name's Joshua. You must be Miss Jenna Ellison."

"No. I'm her younger sister. And it's Winfield. Ellison was my grandfather's name." Her voice was barely audible.

Noticing she hadn't given her first name, he felt like a cat stalking a bird, but didn't want to confront her in front of Barrett. No, better to watch and see what she did. Now that he knew where to find her, he could plan his next move at his leisure.

"I was sorry to hear about your father's passing, Mr Bellinghausen." Her words were directed at Barrett, making Joshua feel as if he were invisible. Her voice rang with determination. "But I'm afraid you've made a trip for nothing. My sister is out of town. You already know what her answer about selling the bull is, but–"

So she was going to play tough to get rid of them. Well, to hell with that. Now that he'd found her, no way was he leaving just yet. The idea that she could so easily dismiss him renewed his anger all over again. "If we could just have a few minutes of your time, ma'am." Joshua stepped forward until Ellie had no choice but to back up and let them in.

Eyes narrowed, she hesitated for a moment. "Fine. If you'll follow me, please." She led them down a dim hallway covered with faded wallpaper and hosting a rogue's gallery of portraits that he assumed were her ancestors, to a bright room that must have once been the parlor.

Ellie took a seat behind an oak desk, fumbled a moment in one of the drawers and slipped a pair of glasses on. Instead of camouflaging her face, as she must have intended, the large, tortoise-shell glasses had the effect of making her eyes look bigger, bluer. Some of his anger slid away, despite his determination to make her squirm.

"Can I offer you a glass of tea?"

Barrett started to shake his head, but Joshua again took charge.

"Thank you, ma'am. That would be very kind of you."

Looking as if she wished she could recall her words, Ellie excused herself to get the refreshments.

"What the hell are you doing?" Barrett sounded distinctly annoyed. "You were just along for the ride. The ranch is my territory, remember? You stay out of my pastures, and I'll stay out of your ice cream."

"I'll explain later."

"You don't need to make a conquest with everything in skirts. Besides, this one probably wears cast-iron panties."

Joshua chuckled. If Barrett only knew, as he would in good time. "They're not. Just play along," he whispered as Ellie returned with a tray and three tall glasses of iced tea garnished with wedges of lemon and sprigs of mint.

Ellie sat in the desk chair and rubbed a finger

down the iced tea glass, following a bead of condensation. Joshua was immediately reminded of what her fingers had felt like moving across his skin. Fine hairs rose on the back of his neck, and heat flooded his groin.

"As I was saying, my sister and I have no intention of selling our prize stock. I understand the situation you find yourselves in, but we're trying to reestablish the reputation of Ellison Farms. We can't do that if we sell off our blue-ribbon breeder. I'm sorry."

Barrett leaned forward. "I admire your plans to turn your grandfather's business back into what it once was, but I'm not sure you fully understand how long that could take. We're here to make you a handsome offer. Sell the bull and turn your efforts to something that will be rewarding in the short term."

"My plans are strictly long-term." Despite her obvious nervousness, Ellie's blue-green eyes hardened to splinters of emerald. "The answer is no, Mr Bellinghausen. And I see no point in discussing it further."

Barrett looked as if he'd like to argue the matter, but Joshua caught his attention. There was no need to push the lady. One way or another, he was certain he could turn her to his way of thinking. The only trouble was, the longer they sat there, Ellie's sweet scent reaching out to him, the more fuzzyheaded he became, until he wasn't certain what his way of thinking was. Or should be.

It was all too easy for him to visualize her delicious curves beneath the shapeless dress. The knit fabric of her shirt clung in the right places. Several buttons were undone, drawing his eyes to where an antique locket nestled demurely. The temperature in the room rose several degrees. He used the napkin to wipe away the sweat that had suddenly popped out on his upper lip. He shifted in his chair.

"Think we could see him anyway, Miss Winfield?" he asked, more for a reason to linger than any real interest. "It will at least give us a better standard to judge the other bulls we've seen today." Naturally, Bellinghausen farms would only want the best, and it was Barrett's job to convince her to sell it to him. Still, he wasn't ready to give up yet.

"He's in the far pasture."

"We've got time, don't we Barrett?"

His younger brother glared at him. "Yeah, sure."

Joshua rose and herded everyone to the Chevy. "We'll just take Barrett's truck." He held the passenger door for Ellie, taking her hand and helping her up into the cab. A frisson of warmth shot through him from the barely perceptible trembling in her fingers. So she was nervous. Good.

Climbing in beside her effectively sandwiched her between him and Barrett. The sensation of her thigh pressed against his made him lightheaded as he recalled the warmth of her bare skin against his. The feeling shot up his leg and settled in the pit of his stomach. "Tell us where."

Her glance told him just where she thought he should go, but she held her head high as she directed Barrett down a rutted trail running along the river past a faded yellow barn. A sheltie ran, barking, alongside the bouncing vehicle. Each bounce of the cab threw her towards him, the softness of her breasts pressing against his arm with each jolt of the truck, making it impossible for him to think of anything but the way she tasted. All too soon she directed Barrett to stop.

Several handsome cows grazed in a pasture next to the road. A dove-gray bull with a splash of white on his wide chest watched with disdain from another fenced in area.

Joshua assisted Ellie from the truck. Walking to the first fence, she hiked her dress up past her knees, climbed up the wooden rails and swung herself over. Caught off guard by the flash of skin and lace, Joshua rubbed a hand across his chin. He had to give her credit, the way she refused to be intimidated by two men who towered over her by more than a foot.

Wind plastered her cotton jumper to her trim body. Joshua hurried across a stretch of buttercups to catch up with her. While he looked on, Ellie extolled the virtues of the bull that had won a blue ribbon at the Blanco County Fair the previous fall.

From his place in the next pasture, the bull observed them with obvious disdain, flaring his nostrils, then turning his back.

As far as Joshua was concerned, a cow was a cow as long as the butterfat content in its milk was up to the dairy standards. And a bull was ... something to be very careful around. He much preferred running the creamery aspect of the business.

Barrett made what Joshua knew to be a very generous offer. Ellie barely stifled a gasp, but vehemently declined.

Barrett shook his head. "I think we've seen enough, don't you, Joshua?"

Not nearly, as far as he was concerned, but could find no reasonable excuse to linger. He'd have to find a way to deal with Miss Winfield later. Several pleasant possibilities occurred to him. What would be the most effective method of resolving this little problem?

"You ready, Joshua?"

He started, realizing his brother had spoken to him several times. "Unless Miss Winfield wants to make a deal on the bull."

She shook her head.

"Well, think on it anyway."

She turned her flinty gaze on him. "I can think on it for the next decade, Mr Bell. The answer will still be no."

Joshua nodded amiably, and they headed back towards the truck. At the fence, when Ellie started to again hike her skirt up, he couldn't resist. Planting his hands on her waist, he picked her up as if she were a doll and set her down on the opposite side, then swung over the rail, returning her outraged expression with a wide grin. He didn't care. Touching her again was worth the indignant look.

"I'll walk back to the house, gentlemen." She stressed the last word. "Please close the gate on your way out."

Joshua paused at the truck. "Got a business card, Barrett?" He kept his voice casual.

Barrett started to say something, then nodded and handed a card to him. After scribbling on the back, Joshua handed it to Ellie, making sure his fingers lingered on hers. She jerked her hand back as if from a cattle brand. The card fluttered to the ground.

Joshua retrieved it and tucked it firmly in her palm. Ellie trembled. "I'll be in touch. Ma'am." Touching the brim of his hat, he climbed inside the cab.

Barrett got in and started the vehicle, accelerating a little faster than necessary out of the farmyard. "What the hell was that all about? Mr Bell?" His face was grim.

Joshua took in a deep breath of the pure spring air. Ah, the sweet taste of victory. Watching Ellie in the side mirror, he couldn't stop the grin that spread across hisface or the sense of satisfaction that flowed through him. "You owe me four grand, little brother."

Chapter Four

Barrett frowned. "Like hell I do."

Joshua gestured behind them. "The initials EW mean anything to you? Well, you've just met Miss Ellie Winfield."

Barrett slammed his palm against the wheel. "Damn you. I knew I shouldn't have asked you to come along. She probably would have sold me the damn bull if you hadn't been here."

Joshua watched her tiny figure become smaller, then the road curved and carried them out of sight. "I don't think so. But I think I can eventually convince her it will be in her best interest to make the deal."

Barrett shot him a dark look. "You're going to blackmail her into selling?"

"Not at all. But I intend to do everything I can to persuade her. Just give me time." He'd let her stew for a few days. That would give him time to get DJ to do a background check. Then he could decide just what was the best way to handle a woman who looked like an innocent fresh from the farm but who traded her virtue for cash.

"Why didn't you tell her who you were?"

"In good time. Maybe. I, for one, have had it with

females who see wedding rings just because they think the family's loaded. I don't want our name clouding her impressions of me."

"Yeah, much better if she thinks of you as a poor lech."

Joshua stretched his legs out and folded his arms across his chest. It didn't matter. He had no long-term intentions as far as Ellie Winfield was concerned. What he had in mind was definitely a lot more fun. A little time alone with her, make that a lot of time alone, with plenty of opportunities for lots of her brand of loving. But first he intended to make her worry just a little.

Yep. He was going to enjoy every minute of this.

Ellie turned the business card over. "You owe me." She gasped. The nerve. That brash, arrogant cowboy thought she owed him. She tossed her head and continued up the road. Well, he could just keep on thinking that. He'd offered to pay her. She hadn't asked. And if she'd ended up with more money than he'd planned on spending that was his problem. The way he'd been all over her, not once, but several times, she'd earned it. The man was an animal, no doubt about it.

Guilty memories of her own pleasure rose unbidden until her face burned. If Joshua Bell was an animal, what did that make *her?*

Unnerved by the implications, Ellie tucked her

mother's old reading glasses in her pocket. They hadn't stopped him from recognizing her; they'd only made her dizzy and off center.

Wondering what he was planning, sick with worry over the possibilities, she walked back up the lane. Warm April sunshine beat on the top of her bare head. What if he called her? What would she do?

When Jenna called later from Cleveland, Ellie sat curled up in the wicker rocker on the porch, still trying to sort through what had happened. He hadn't confronted her in front of Barrett Bellinghausen at least. Probably to save his own hide. What employee wanted their boss to know they'd paid a woman to have sex? The thought struck her that he'd been carrying around a lot of money, especially for a ranch foremen. What if it had been his entire paycheck? His life's savings? Or worse, what if it hadn't even been his money? She completely missed Jenna's question.

"You said Barrett Bellinghausen came by. How did it go?"

"Like you'd expect," she lied, not wanting Jenna to have more to worry about.

"He's very handsome, isn't he?" Jenna's voice sounded wistful.

"Is he? I didn't notice." She hadn't, either. Focused so totally on Joshua and terrified of what he was going to do or say, she couldn't remember anything about Barrett, except he had been nearly as tall as her cowboy.

"Shame on you, Ellie. Thirty-two is too young not to notice a man as attractive as Barrett. He thinks I'm some kind of kook, just because I'm an artist, but I would think you'd find some common ground with him. You know, the cows and all that breeding stuff."

"If I were looking for a man, which I'm not any more than you are, I'd prefer one who could discuss something other than the merits of one breed of heifers over another."

Jenna sighed. "I guess you're right."

"How's Lauren?" Ellie hurriedly changed the subject.

"Settling in. I rented some video games to get us through until her first doctor's appointment tomorrow. Speaking of doctors, have you made your appointment with Taylor yet?"

"I'll call her office first thing in the morning."

"Be sure you do," Jenna warmed to her role as elder sister. "I've been worried about you lately."

"I'm fine. Just not sleeping too good the past few weeks. Worrying about Lauren, the money and everything else." Not to mention the recurring erotic dreams she'd had since her night with Joshua. The one where she lay curled against him, spoon fashion, was particularly vivid, as if she had actually made love with him that way, yet she knew she hadn't. Because if she had, the potential for disaster was enormous. She quickly stifled the thoughts before panic had a chance to take root.

"I'll call Taylor in the morning. I promise."

Jenna said goodbye, then put Lauren on the phone for a brief chat. A few minutes later, Ellie hung up the phone. Tucked into the rocker, she rested her chin on her knees. Her imagination hadn't exaggerated how handsome Joshua was. Why would a man who looked like that pay for sex?

Of course, he'd said it was the first time he had, but why should she believe him? Maybe if he hadn't been so drunk, he would have wanted her to do something dreadfully kinky involving silk scarves. Or boots and spurs.

She knew she had little concept of romantic entanglements. Absorbed in biology since she was Lauren's age, she was so thoroughly grounded in the physiology of sex that she'd never been able to understand the pure sensuality of the act. She'd never met a man who could make her look beyond the notion that you put tab A into slot B and voila, nature's cycle continued.

Until she'd met Joshua. The feelings he stirred in her had been as unexpected as snow in the Hill Country.

She rocked, thinking, and pushing one bare foot against the cool wooden floor of the porch. It was just as well she'd taken a self-imposed vow of celibacy, since one taste of lovemaking left her thirsting for what she knew she couldn't have. She couldn't risk getting pregnant. There was no way she'd put a child through what Lauren's life had been like, and she knew she could never bear to watch from the sidelines again, either.

The next day, she scheduled her doctor's appointment for several days later with her physician, a friend from college who'd gone on to establish her own practice in Austin. She hated having to depend on Taylor's charity just to have a medical exam, but she couldn't even afford the deductible on the basic medical insurance she had through work, let alone the cost of paying for a routine check-up. Necessity won out over her pride.

Using the address on Barrett's business card, she mailed the money clip to Joshua. Let him tell her now she owed him something.

For the next few days, each time the phone rang, she nearly jumped out of her skin, but Joshua didn't call. Jenna checked in and reported that Lauren's tests were going well, and they expected to be home in another week.

Her thoughts returned to her cowboy. Joshua had just been toying with her the other day, trying to frazzle her nerves. The thought filled her with anger, but she breathed a little easier as each day wound down. There was hope for Lauren. She'd done the right thing, but now it was time to forget about it.

By the end of the third day, she'd finally relaxed.

He wasn't going to call. He'd gotten what he wanted, and she could go on in peace.

Joshua rolled the money clip in his hand. So she wasn't as dishonest as he'd thought. Too bad she hadn't returned three quarters of the money she'd taken, but with the four grand Barrett owed him, he'd lost interest in the cash Ellie had cost him. No, there was really only one thing she still owed him, and he wanted it badly.

She owed him the rest of a night. The more he thought about what it would be like to make love to her all night long, then wake up with her head on his pillow, the more he wanted it, until the need took on a life of its own. DJ 's report had turned up a profile of a woman who was a complete contradiction to his initial impression of her.

A high school biology teacher, for pete's sake. A respected member of the small Hill Country community where her family had lived for over a hundred years.

He picked up her gold compact. EW. The metal case warmed in his palm, reminding him of how Ellie's silken skin had heated beneath his touch. He wanted her all right. One more time.

Once he got her out of his system, he could concentrate on the difficult problem of finding a suitable wife and settling down to the terms of Dad's will.

But first he needed to rid himself of the fantasy of being with Ellie again. He reached for the phone. It was time to collect the debt.

Ellie had just sat down with a glass of homemade wine and a low-fat microwave lasagna dinner when the phone rang. She laid her fork down and waited. Jenna had already called, so it couldn't be her. Unless it was bad news.

Releasing an anxious breath, she went to answer the kitchen extension. "Hello?"

"This is a collect call."

Ellie's heart thumped wildly. Joshua Bell, his voice as intoxicating as a snifter of warm brandy. She had hoped . . . . Torn between wishing she could be with him again and knowing it was the worst thing for her, she wasn't sure what she had hoped for. "What if I don't want to accept the charges?"

His sexy laugh sent a wild thrill of anticipation bubbling through her.

"You struck me as the type of lady who keeps her word. So I figured whatever made you run off like that just meant you planned to make it up to me some other time."

Ellie twisted the phone cord around her hand. He wanted to see her again? "I'm not a, I don't usually—I mean I can't give the money back. At least not right now." She swallowed and hurried on. "I didn't intend to take any more than you had promised me. I swear I'll pay it back as soon as I'm able."

"It's not the money I'm interested in."

Two thousand dollars? That was difficult to believe. What kind of man was he? Ellie sank into a chair. "What then?" she whispered.

"I want to see you again. Only this time as two people who want to get to know each other a little better."

"I can't."

"Married?"

"Of course not!"

"Then what's the problem?" His voice was soothing, persuasive.

"I can't afford an entanglement." That was an understatement, she told herself, covering her face with one hand.

His low chuckle reminded her of just how much she had cost him, and the feeling of obligation filled her with shame. Her face flooded with warmth.

"Me, either. How about we take it one night at a time?"

Hearing his voice, she could close her eyes and be back in the motel room she couldn't much remember because she'd been so focused on him. She could, however, recall in vivid detail how he'd touched her, and the way she'd felt, the good parts far outweighing the bad. Did she want to run off for an evening of bliss with the most sinfully gorgeous man she'd ever met?

With every particle of her being.

"You owe me, darlin', but I can't make you do anything you don't want to do."

Why did he have to keep reminding her? Pride made her stiffen her spine. She'd be damned before she'd owe anyone anything. Especially a man.

At least he hadn't embarrassed her in front of Barrett Bellinghausen. He *had* come to her rescue at Dandy Don's Danceland. It wasn't his fault he'd gotten caught up in her desperate scheme. She was lucky she'd ended up with him. Alternative scenarios played out in her mind, each one more terrifying than the one before.

One night. What could it hurt? Then she'd no longer feel guilty and obligated. She'd be free.

"Ellie," he whispered in his damnably seductive voice. "When?"

Closing her eyes, she made the decision in an instant, before logic and rationality could stop her. "I'm going to be in Austin day after tomorrow. It would probably be a good idea for me to stay the night."

There, she'd taken the first step. If he didn't think it was worth driving into Austin, then that was his tough luck. There was no way she'd risk spending the night with him anywhere near her home or his, assuming he lived near Belle Ranch, which she knew was east of Austin.

"Perfect. I need to take care of some business there myself. Call me on my mobile phone," he gave her the number, "and I'll tell you where to meet me. I promise it won't be the Lamplighter."

Remembering how his hands had felt on her, she didn't much care if it was. "Okay."

"And Ellie? Don't disappoint me."

Despite the warmth in his voice, she detected an undercurrent of resolve that might have been a threat. She shivered. He could ruin her reputation in this small town. She didn't want that, for Lauren and Jenna's sake as much as for her own.

"'Til Friday, then." She carefully hung up the phone. Hoping she wasn't making another terrible mistake, yet sure that she was, she returned to the dining room to find the lasagna had congealed into a pool of cold cheese and tough noodles. Wrinkling her nose, she scraped it into the garbage can.

The wine she downed in a single gulp.

Friday afternoon, Ellie sat in the waiting room of her doctor's office and picked up the current issue of *Texas Monthly*. A picture of Wilmer Bellinghausen filled the cover. "The End of a Dynasty?" the caption proclaimed.

Sounded like something she'd heard before. He didn't look as old as she would have expected for someone who had been one of Texas' most successful businessmen, but then he was Barrett's father, and Barrett was probably close to her own age. She was checking the table of contents for the page number of the accompanying article when her name was called. She set the magazine back on the glass coffee table. No sense in starting to read something she wouldn't have time to finish. She probably wouldn't be able to concentrate on a word since her meeting with Joshua had her pulse beating in triple time.

A few minutes later, Ellie, wrapped in a blue paper gown, sat in the examining room. Taylor's framed certificates hung on the wall. Pride flashed through Ellie for her friend and what she had accomplished.

Dr Taylor Hunnicutt entered, gave her a warm smile and a hug. "Ellie! So good to see you. You look terrific."

Ellie gestured at the sheet covering her legs and grinned at her former college roommate. "You always manage to catch me looking my best." She clapped a hand to her forehead. "I forgot your dress."

Taylor shrugged. "That's okay. I don't get much of a chance to wear slinky black dresses myself." She rang for her assistant, then snapped on latex gloves. "Let's take care of business, then we can chat."

A few minutes later, the exam complete, the nurse left. Taylor reviewed Ellie's chart and patted her knee.

"I'm very relieved to tell you that unlike last time, everything looks normal." She winked. "I'm so glad you finally got it on with someone, Ellie. I was beginning to think we were going to have to have you bronzed."

"Oh, really? Here stands the last American virgin?"

"Of our generation, anyway." Taylor's eyes twinkled. "Tell me about him. Is he wonderful? Does this mean you've changed your mind about getting married someday?"

Ellie was horrified. "No! I mean, it's not serious. It's just sex, for heaven's sake."

"Hmmm." Taylor looked unconvinced. "That sounds like our Ellie. I hope you're practicing safe sex at least."

"Naturally. I do have a nodding acquaintance with biology, remember."

Taylor laughed. "Maybe, but I've never met anyone else so uninterested in the human aspect of it." She started to say something, then bit her lip. "I'm going to do some blood work this time. Check your cholesterol and all that other good stuff."

Ellie nodded. She'd expected that when she'd made the appointment.

"Hop down and get dressed, then see Dracula's bride, my blood-thirsty nurse." She paused on her way out. "I wish I would have known sooner you were coming in. I would have loved to meet you for lunch. You going back tonight?"

Ellie couldn't quite meet her eyes. "I'll probably do a little shopping, then go home. Hungry cows await me. Next time, okay?"

"Deal." Taylor waved and shut the door behind her.

Ellie let out a breath. That's all she needed was for Taylor to start meddling around in who her mysterious boyfriend was.

How could she tell her she didn't really know that herself?

Chapter Five

He couldn't stop smiling. Joshua smoothed a comb through his hair and grinned. Tonight he'd be with Ellie. He'd solve the enigma. Then the gnawing feeling of unfinished business would finally be gone.

Whistling, he tossed his shaving kit into his gym bag and looked up to see Barrett standing in the bedroom door.

"Why are you so disgustingly cheerful this morning? Could it have something to do with that overnight bag you're packing?"

"I've got a business meeting in Austin this afternoon. I expect it to run very late."

"I take it you'd like me to inform our mothers you'll be gone overnight."

"Would you? I'd appreciate it." Joshua straightened the turquoise slide on his string tie and settled his black Stetson on his head.

"Anyone I know?"

"Actually, I think you've met her only once. Just last week as a matter of fact."

Barrett's jaw dropped. "Get out of town. You're not meeting Ellie Winfield?"

"That's the one."

"Why? Besides the obvious fact that she's not your type."

Joshua narrowed his gaze on him but refused to let Barrett dampen his high spirits. "My type being?"

"Something a little more exotic than a plain, pinch-butt woman who looks like she is someone's high school principal, that's what your type is."

Ellie plain? Joshua arched a brow. "You're either losing your eyesight or getting entirely too attached to those stupid cows. Besides, you'd know Ellie was a knockout if you'd seen her the way I have, although I'm glad you haven't. And she owes me, damn it."

"I don't know what the hell happened between you." Barrett sighed. "I mean, I know, I just don't understand. Something is wrong with this picture."

"She's obviously over the age of consent."

Barrett folded his arms and gave him a stony look. "Our grandfathers did business together, did you know that? She's a nice lady, Joshua. I hope you realize what you're doing."

"Relax. I've got it under control."

"So you say." Shaking his head, Barrett pushed away from the doorjamb and left.

Refusing to take Barrett's gloomy words seriously, Joshua set off for Austin. Blue skies promised a glorious day. Fields of bluebonnets and Indian paintbrush dotted the grass alongside the highway. So Ellie Winfield had somehow managed to arouse the infamous Bellinghausen protective instincts in his little brother. Well, at least Joshua could take comfort in knowing he wasn't the only one she affected that way.

Later, business meetings concluded, Joshua stood on the balcony of his well-appointed suite at the Four Seasons Hotel, glass of wine in hand. Ellie had called a short time ago. She was going to go through with it. He hadn't realized how worried he'd been that she might back out until he'd heard her soft voice on the phone. Taut with anticipation, he exhaled slowly, sipped the wine and considered how he wanted the evening to go.

Suddenly, it was very important that everything be just right. He should have made a dinner reservation somewhere really elegant, told her to wear a nice dress. That little black silky thing would have been good. He should have ….

In her borrowed high heels, Ellie stepped across the uneven Mexican tile of the lobby at the Four Seasons Hotel and tried not to look as awed as she felt. What a gorgeous place, something Joshua would like with it's Southwestern style and colors. Steer horns adorned the walls. An enormous bouquet of Texas wildflowers graced a polished antique table in the center of the lobby.

Attention diverted, she wobbled on the tile and nearly lost her grip on her tapestry tote. Contrary to

Austin's casual chic style of dress, the patrons of the Four Seasons looked polished and professional. Ladies in silk business suits sat with equally elegantly clad men in the lobby bar sipping cocktails.

In Blanco, Jenna's lovely handmade fashions were more than adequate, and Ellie never thought much about the impression she made in her homemade dresses. She'd never felt so awkward and out of place as she did now. At least not since the first time she'd seen Joshua.

She scurried to the brass doors of the elevator, wanting nothing more than to avoid the curious stares. She couldn't wait to get to the anonymity of the room. Why had she agreed to this?

He hurried to answer the rap at the door. Ellie stood there, a soft, flowery print dress floating past her knees, pretty, but covering too damn much of her. She clutched a small satchel as if it contained everything she held dear in the world.

"The lamb to the slaughter," she joked.

Joshua laughed and held the door for her to enter. "Oh, not the slaughter, surely. Just maybe the big bad wolf."

When she entered the room, her heel caught on the plush carpet, pitching her towards him, forcing him to save her from what could have been a bad fall. Her soft curves pressing against him felt so good, so familiar, he held her a bit longer than necessary. Just to make sure she hadn't turned her ankle. "Whoa. You okay?"

She eased away from him. "Fine." A faint pink crept up her neck. "So you're the big bad wolf?"

"To hear Barrett talk, one would think so. Can I get you a glass of wine?"

She nodded and set the bag down near the door. In case she changed her mind and wanted to make a quick getaway? Not wanting to take a chance, he picked it up and carried it to the bedroom, setting it just inside. When he returned, he noticed she'd removed her shoes.

"Why would Mr Bellinghausen talk to you that way?"

Pouring a glass of wine at the bar located in the corner of the living room, he hesitated, splashing a little wine on the gray marble counter. Shit. She still didn't realize who he was. Well, he wasn't about to enlighten her. At least not yet. "Oh, we go way back."

He handed her a goblet and tapped the crystal with his. "To tonight?"

"Tonight," she echoed and took a sip of wine, her eyes very blue and luminous over the rim of the goblet. Blonde hair framed her face, flowed in golden waves over her shoulders. His gut tightened. She was beautiful. Why hadn't he remembered how fragilely pretty she was? She made the women he usually dated look like Amazons.

Wanting to touch her, but knowing he had to wait until she lost the slightly trapped expression she wore, he smiled. "We can still catch a bit of the sunset from the balcony."

Ellie smiled. "I'd like that."

Taking her hand, he led her past the bedroom to the sliding glass doors. She cast a nervous glance at the king-size bed, and he nearly chuckled. Man, she was edgy. She ought to remember from the other night that she didn't have anything to worry about.

He stood beside her at the rail, close, but not quite touching. "I understand you're a biology teacher."

She gave him a startled look. "How did you know that?"

"Barrett told me. He's met your sister."

"I planned to do genetic research after I graduated, but I like teaching. The kids are a lot of fun. Most of the time."

Her gaze drifted to the Colorado River nine stories below. "So what do you do at Bellinghausen's?"

"Eat a lot of ice cream," he joked.

Ellie shot him a quick look. "I thought you said you were the ranch foreman."

Oops. "Yeah, well, everyone there eats a lot of ice cream. It's a job requirement. If you don't like ice cream, you don't get hired. I mean, sometimes I help Barrett out at the ranch. Sometimes I'm at the creamery. I'm in charge of butter brickle."

"I see," she said, although it was obvious from

the little frown creasing her forehead that she didn't.

"Would you like to go out for dinner?" he asked, more to change the subject than from any real desire to leave the room now that he had her alone again.

"Maybe later. I'm not really hungry."

Well, he was. Ravenous, actually, but only for her. In fact, if he didn't touch her, at least a little, his nerves would be stretched to the point where he was sure to rush things the way he had the first night. Taking her glass, he set it on the patio table.

Ellie looked up at him. She gestured at her dress. "I mean, I'm not really dressed for this place."

"You're right. You're much too pretty."

A pulse fluttered in her throat, like a captured butterfly beating its wings frantically. He brushed his knuckle down her cheek, felt her tremble.

"Are you afraid of me, Ellie?"

"Of course not." But her gaze skittered away from his.

He feathered the back of his fingers over her face, down her throat, then slid his hand to the back of her neck and caressed. She half-closed her eyes and sighed. "Did I hurt you in some way and I don't even know it?"

"No!"

He let out a breath. He'd been concerned that the booze had made him overly amorous, and she was so tiny, so delicate. "Good. I promise, anything you don't want to do, just say so."

"Okay."

She swayed a little towards him and didn't pull away when he cupped his palms on her shoulders. "I don't feel like talking right now." She hesitated.

He held his breath, half-afraid of what she'd say. "What's on your mind, Ellie?"

"What do you want from me?"

Only everything. Now. "It would be nice if you'd relax."

"I'll try."

He lightly stroked her back. She moved a little closer into his embrace, almost as if she were unaware of what she was doing. She tilted her head back. Blue-green eyes met his, the longing and apprehension in her gaze nearly bowling him over.

"Maybe if you'd kiss me?" her words were a silky whisper.

"Good plan," he murmured, cupping her face in his hands, and lowering his mouth to hers. His lips moved slowly over hers, tasting, teasing. She was so sweet. She clasped his wrists, as if she were afraid he would stop kissing her. As if he could.

Man, she was short. Although it would be worth it, he'd never stand up straight again, if they kept at it like this. Uttering a frustrated oath, he settled his hands on her waist and lifted her against him, wrapping his arms around her and clasping her tightly. Ellie giggled and draped her arms around his shoulders.

Her mouth came down hard on his. A jolt of pure passion shot through him when she nipped his lip, then swirled her tongue against his. This he remembered, the hot temptation of her. The unbridled passion she drew from him.

The need to feel her skin fogged his mind. His hand crept up her dress, slid along the silken skin of her thighs. He squeezed her buttocks and groaned. "Any chance we can take this party inside before my body overrides my brain and I make love to you right here?"

She drew in a quick breath, but didn't look nearly as shocked as he'd expected. A little spark flared in her eyes which told him she found the idea of making love on a balcony as erotic as he did.

"You're wicked."

"I try." Holding her tightly, he carried her inside, leaving the doors open to the cool, spring night and tumbled onto the bed with her.

Lying on her back, Ellie gazed up at him as he stretched out beside her. Still a bit scared about what would happen next, she reached up and touched his face. Part of her wanted to hurry and get it over with before she lost her nerve. The rest of her wanted the magic to never end.

Joshua captured her fingers and kissed them. Her heart jumped. When he looked at her that way, his eyes heated and intense, the rest of the world ceased to exist. All the problems, all the doubts vanished. Warmth spread inside her, like slow burning coals carefully stirred to a quick hot blaze, incinerating the last of her defenses.

He dropped little kisses on the tip of her nose, across her face, down her throat to the first button on the very long row running down her dress. His hands moved caressingly over her, making her feel as if he touched her everywhere at once.

"Ellie," he whispered against her skin. "I want you to undress me."

She raised herself on one elbow and began working the bolero loose. Setting the turquoise clip on the nightstand, she slowly undid the pearl buttons on his western shirt and slid it down his arms. She combed her fingers through the soft, springy hair on his chest. Dark brown and silky, it formed a trail she followed to his belt buckle.

His tongue traced the outline of her ear, and he whispered softly, making her toes curl. She rested her fingertips against his chest and closed her eyes. If she'd only known how things could be between a man and woman, she might have been tempted a long time ago to break the vow she'd made when her mother died.

After tonight, she'd never see Joshua again. But she wouldn't think about that now. She was entitled to one night, wasn't she?

Moving from the shelter of his arms, she tugged his boots off, then the black jeans and socks. This time he wasn't wearing plain white briefs as he had the other night, but sexy, black bikinis. She hooked her fingers in the sides and pulled them off, kissing her way down his legs as she did so.

Joshua groaned and opened his eyes. "Too much more of that and we'll never get your clothes off."

"Tell me when you want me to stop," she murmured. Intoxicated by his reaction, she kissed the flat plane of his abdomen, then swirled her tongue in his navel. The thought of him being deliciously naked while she was still fully clothed made her feel giddily in control.

"I'll let you know in a month or two." He gripped her by the forearms and pulled her up his body. Shifting her to her back, he captured her mouth with his.

His fingers nimbly worked the tiny buttons on her dress, one after another until the dress opened all the way down. Sliding one arm behind her back and lifting her slightly, he tugged the dress away and tossed it to the floor. Lacy white panties and bra followed. One huge hand cupped her breast, while the other made lazy circles on her stomach.

His eyes darkened. "I was too drunk the other night to truly appreciate you. I apologize."

Heat floated over her skin, as much from embarrassment as from arousal. "It's okay."

"No, it's not. You need to be savored." He lowered his head and pulled one rosy nipple into his mouth.

Ellie felt herself being drawn tighter and tighter as his tongue and lips worshipped one breast, then the other. His hand drifted over the curve of her hips, then lower. Stroking the inside of her thigh, his hand crept higher. She instinctively moved closer, craving his intimate touch, whimpering for it, until at last his fingers delved inside. She molded into the curve of his hand.

"I need you to touch me, Ellie," he whispered against her mouth.

She curved her hands over his shoulders, smoothed over his chest, his belly, down into the thatch of hair. Her fingers trembled over the smooth, hot length of his erection, but this time it was from the aching desire building in her. She stroked the silky heat.

Joshua groaned and nipped her shoulder. Pulling her tightly against him, he rolled to the edge of the bed and removed a foil packet from the drawer of the bedside table.

Lying on his back, he sheathed himself, then settled her over his hips. The first tremors of intense excitement hit her as he eased inside. She shifted her position slightly, relishing the freedom to move however she wanted, enjoying the power she held to make his breath hitch.

Joshua gripped her hips, rocking into her, then followed the slow, lazy rhythm she set.

Ellie closed her eyes, luxuriating in the powerful feel of him inside her. If this was heaven, she never wanted to leave and if it wasn't . . .

He slid his hand between their bodies, his fingers expertly caressing her with the same easy pace she had set until the fever grew. She breathed his name.

Moving faster, she took him in, letting him go, then bringing him back, while he stroked faster, thrusting into her until he shouted her name and the world whirled away.

Hours later, Ellie curled against his side, reveling in the feel of his hands softly stroking her skin. Her fingers danced down to the throbbing evidence that he was more than ready for her again. "Anyone ever tell you there's a chance you might be oversexed?"

He sucked in a breath. "My brother. Constantly."

"And how does he know this?" She watched his face, although with his eyes closed, it was difficult to read anything into his expression but contentment.

"Hero worship, I guess." He opened his eyes and grinned at her. "I don't have the heart to tell him he's been misled."

"I disagree," she murmured, moving her hands over him, loving the way he pulsed against her palm. She felt him studying her intently.

"Why me, Ellie?"

"Why you what?"

"You know what I mean. You were a virgin."

So he'd figured it out, despite her efforts to make him think otherwise. "Who says I was?"

He made an impatient gesture. "Several very obvious signs. What made you do it?"

She bristled with defensiveness. No way was she

going to tell him the real reason. "I'm thirty-two. It was past time. My gynecologist was threatening to have me bronzed."

He frowned, obviously not satisfied with her answer. She continued stroking him. Her own desire building to an ache, she trailed little kisses down his body, yearning to please him the way he'd pleased her.

"Trying to distract me?"

"Umm, hmm." She ran her tongue over the silky length of him. "Am I?"

"That'll do it." His words sounded strangled. He gripped her shoulders when she took the tip in her mouth. "Ellie!"

Taking her hand, he wrapped her fingers around him, showing her how he liked best to be touched.

Ellie wriggled against his leg, surprised how thoroughly arousing it was to know she was bringing him to a fever pitch with her hands and mouth. Reaching for her, he pulled her up to him and shifted her to her back. He fumbled with the foil packet, then he was sinking deep inside her and moaning her name.

Ellie tightened around him, loving the way it made him close his eyes and draw a ragged breath.

"Bonus points for being a fast learner." Bracing himself, his arms bracketing her shoulders, he withdrew partway, then glided inside, watching the way she bit her lip, the way her eyes fluttered shut, the way it looked to be joined with her. The moment burned into his brain, setting him on fire and sapping his control until he was thrusting faster, riding out the torrent and taking her with him.

Chapter Six

Up to her neck in bubble bath, Ellie let Joshua feed her a mouthful of Mama Belle's strawberry cheesecake ice cream. "You are without a doubt the most decadent person I've ever known."

"That's only because you lead an incredibly sheltered life."

Ellie scowled. "I have a master's in biology, and I've lived on a farm most of my life. I think I know about the birds and bees."

"Maybe." Sitting across from her in the tub, his long legs drawn up, cowboy hat perched on the back of his head, he fed her another spoonful from the half-pint carton and grinned. "But you were clueless about what goes on between a man and a woman until you met me."

"Such arrogance." She splashed a handful of bubbles at him.

He raised a brow. "You're going to deny it?"

"Yes, if only to keep that head of yours a size that will allow you to still wear your Stetson."

"I'm serious, Ellie. I want to know what you were doing in that dump. Why you went with me. What you needed the money for."

She couldn't let the cold reality of her life intrude

on her only night of mind dizzying passion. He'd said he only wanted this one night. He had no right to start prying. She didn't want his pity any more than she'd wanted his anger.

Staring into the bubbles, Ellie took a deep breath. "I understand your curiosity. But really. It's none of your business." Looking up, she met the flinty determination in his gaze. "You promised I wouldn't have to do anything I didn't want to do."

He made an impatient noise. "What I meant was–"

"You said anything. Well, I don't want to talk about this. And I won't." She stared into his eyes, refusing to back down. Joshua sighed. A tiny spark of admiration lit his gaze.

"Damn if you aren't one determined lady. Okay, darlin'. If that's what you want. But it's not going to stop me from wondering."

"That's not all I want." She took another bite of ice cream and got to her knees, wedging herself between his thighs and kissing him. Tasting like strawberries and cream, his tongue swirled around hers.

The carton and spoon fell to the tile floor. Joshua's arms came around her, pressing her breasts against his damp chest. His hands roving down her bottom, he nibbled on her ear.

"Like I said, whatever you want."

Early morning light drifted in on the cool breeze through the open balcony door. Joshua watched Ellie sleep. He liked the way her hair looked against his pillow, the way her lower lip looked all pouty, like she was dreaming of kisses.

His arm tightened around her. His kisses. Knowing that he was the first man, the only man, she'd made love with filled him with ridiculous pride.

He wanted to know more about her, he didn't understand why. Damn if she wasn't the most close-mouthed woman he'd ever met. Not that it mattered. As they'd agreed, they'd never see each other again after tonight. It was what they both wanted.

Right.

Not wanting the night to end too soon, he took the receiver off the phone and stuck it in the drawer, just in case. Not even Barrett knew where he was, but his brother could be quite a bloodhound sometimes. He didn't want him showing up with a cup of coffee this time.

He sank further under the covers, hugging Ellie close to his side. Something about her freshness appealed immensely to him. Which just showed how jaded he'd become. It would wear thin, eventually, like the other women always did.

Ellie snuggled closer, draping her arm over his waist and pressing against his thigh. She murmured in her sleep and smiled when he pressed a kiss to her temple.

His heart flipped over.

Somehow, the ache he'd carried in his soul since the day Dad died faded when he was with her. He'd had a need. She'd fulfilled it. So he'd never see her again. So what?

He had enough of his own problems. She was one peculiar woman. Secretive, innocent, and world weary all at once. By the time they parted later, he planned to have her completely out of his system.

They lingered over a late room-service breakfast. Joshua's intentions to leave in the morning had disappeared with the dawn, leaving him searching for creative reasons why Ellie should stay. For a while longer, anyway.

She held up her hands to ward him off. "Enough already! I can't take anymore."

Joshua put the spoonful of praline ice cream in his own mouth. "Don't you like ice cream?"

"Yes, but I think I've eaten a years supply in the past twenty-four hours. How many cartons did you bring?"

He shrugged and polished off the pint container. "I didn't know what your favorite flavor is, so I brought a variety." He pulled the cover off the specially designed cooler packed with dry ice and two remaining cartons. "You take them home. Which one did you like best?"

She groaned. "All of them. None of them. You

keep the rest. I've probably gained ten pounds already."

"Not a chance. But if it makes you feel more virtuous, we could go for a walk by the lake."

Ellie pulled the white terry robe with the Four Seasons insignia closer. "Virtuous is the last thing I'm feeling. I think I'd rather take a nap."

Taking her hands, he pulled her up off the sofa. "Come on lazy bones. Let's get some sunshine. Then we can have lunch before heading for home."

"I'll agree to a walk, but no more food. I don't usually eat much."

He cupped her face in his hands and dropped a light kiss on her mouth. "Then I'll have your share."

The afternoon began to fade, and finally Joshua couldn't find another reason to delay leaving. Well, actually he could, but Ellie insisted she needed to get home, and he was certain she was as wiped out as he was.

He wondered if she was also as content.

A short time later, he loaded the cooler of ice cream into her truck and slammed it shut. "Are you sure this thing is reliable?"

"Certainly." Ellie bristled. The ancient pickup wasn't much to look at, but it had been as faithful as an old friend.

He eyed the truck, his expression full of doubt. "It'll be dark by the time you get home. I'll follow you, make sure you don't have any problems."

"Joshua, that's ridiculous. You need to go east. I

live west. How can Blanco possibly be on your way home?"

He placed his hands on her shoulders and studied her face as if he wanted to tell her something, but couldn't find the words. Finally, he pulled her close and rested his cheek against her hair.

She sighed, the slight irritation she felt over his protective attitude fading away under his tender regard. Wrapping her arms around his waist, she wished she never had to let go. His heart thumped a reassuring rhythm.

"Humor me, Ellie." His voice was husky, like fine brandy.

She stood on tiptoe and accepted his kiss. "Okay. This time. But you've got to understand there's no way my vehicle is up to the speed of yours. You start getting impatient, I won't mind if you turn around and head east."

"I won't. Now scoot, before–I'll see you later."

Ellie got in her truck and buckled the belt, wondering what he'd been about to say. It didn't matter. Once they reached Blanco, they'd say goodbye and that would be the end of it.

Soft twilight dusted the fields as she pulled off the county road onto the gravel lane and stopped by the mailbox. Beyond the house, a single star winked in a smoky-blue sky streaked with fading pink and orange. She walked back to the Jaguar as Joshua climbed out.

"I take it this is as far as I go?"

Her gaze skittered away. "My neighbor's been taking care of the stock for me. I don't want to have to explain you, in case he's still around."

"I understand. I think." He pulled her close, stroking his hands down her back.

She had the feeling he didn't want to let her go anymore than she wanted him to. But they had to part. "So, are we even now?" She rested her palms on his chest, trying for a teasing tone to lighten the suddenly somber mood. Smiling, she tilted her head to see his expression.

"Hell no."

"Joshua!"

He grinned and bent his head to brush a kiss against her mouth. "I definitely owe you."

"I'll let you know if I decide to collect."

His expression turned serious, the heat in his gaze making her tremble. "You do that, Ellie."

Then his mouth covered hers, stealing her breath, weakening her knees, and shaking the foundations of the wall she'd built so carefully around her heart.

By the time Joshua reached Austin, the halfway point between his home and hers, he'd thought of a hundred reasons why he shouldn't see Ellie again.

When he passed the outskirts on the east side of Austin and neared Belle Ranch, he'd discounted every reason except one.

He needed a wife and Ellie Winfield just wasn't

marriage material.

How could she be indifferent about giving up her virginity? Not that the state of her chastity was an issue. He'd lost his so long ago, he could barely remember why he had felt such a driving need to let it go.

Ellie was different. She had been saving herself for an awfully long time, why would she give it up so casually? It made him wonder about her beliefs, her attitudes, her morals.

No, the only way to find out how she really felt about it, now that she knew how to get in touch with him, was to wait and let her call him. Which, if he had a clue at all about someone's instinctive attachment to a first lover, she would.

Still, it wouldn't hurt to send flowers.

Glad to have a plan, he arrived at the ranch relaxed and content.

Until he entered the house and realized the mommas had invited company to dinner, and he was two hours late.

Barrett greeted him at the door, a drink in hand and a grim look on his face. "At last. Reinforcements."

Joshua set his gym bag on the bottom step of the floating staircase. "What's going on?"

Barrett tossed back half of his drink in one gulp. "Imagine, if you will, a determined mother, dead set on marrying off her sons. Now multiply that by five."

"Ah, shit."

"My thoughts exactly. Come in and meet the Brickmayer sisters, both of whom look alarmingly like what Ellie Winfield didn't want to sell me the other day."

He got an immediate picture of the taciturn bull in Ellie's pasture and let out a loud guffaw.

Barrett scowled. "Try to act sleepy even though you've spent the past twenty-four hours in bed, would you? I've just about got the sisters convinced we're both early to bed, early to rise, kind of guys."

Joshua let himself be led into the parlor, although all he wanted was a cool shower and time to think about last night. And Ellie.

Barrett introduced him to Lisa and Lori Brickmayer, identical twins, who although they seemed very nice, did exhibit some of the broad, bland features of Ellie's blue-ribbon bull.

Rosemary, stepmom #1, beamed at him. "You missed dinner, but I'd be happy to fix you a plate."

"No thanks, Rosemary." He accepted a drink from Barrett and forced himself to join the desultory conversation until he decided he'd carried out his duty to be polite to the mommas' guests. He swallowed a yawn and made his apologies. "Long day. I hope y'all will excuse me."

After helping Barrett finish the goodnights, he made his way to his room. A short time later, Joshua lay on his back staring at the ceiling. A cool breeze drifted in through the open window. The yard light sent a feeble glow into the room. Patterns flickered on the ceiling from the trees just barely budding outside his window.

He glanced at the bedside clock. Eleven p.m. The house had quieted an hour ago. Ellie might still be awake. She hadn't said where the rest of her family was. Hell, she hadn't even said whom her family included, except for her older sister, but the darkened house had indicated no one else was home. Maybe she needed someone to talk to.

He reached for the phone, the thought of hearing her voice sending heat coiling in his belly.

Chapter Seven

Ellie answered on the third ring, her sleepy voice sharp edged with anxiety. "Hello?"

"It's me. Joshua."

Joshua? Wide-awake, Ellie leaned over and switched on the bedside lamp.

"Were you awake?"

"Well, I am now." Actually, she had been lying there for an hour staring at the ceiling, but there was no way she was going to admit that to him. Especially since the sound of his voice filled her with a deep yearning that nibbled away at her resolve to remain unaffected by their last encounter. She'd been taking care of an obligation, how much she enjoyed being with him didn't matter. She wrapped one arm around her waist, as if that would keep the longing inside.

"Sorry. I just thought–"

The uncertainty in his voice surprised her. She relented. "It's okay. I hadn't fallen asleep yet."

"I wanted to give you a couple of numbers. In case you ever need to call me."

She couldn't imagine why he thought she'd ever do that, but the need to reassure him about whatever bothered him tugged at her. Maybe he felt guilty about being so adamant over never seeing her again. How ironic, when she was equally determined that her second encounter with Joshua Bell would be the last one. "Okay."

"You say that a lot. You know?"

Ellie piled her pillows behind her back and leaned against the headboard. "I'm a middle child. I'm a born pleaser."

"You're really good at it, too." The suggestiveness in his voice made her face flood with warmth. "It's one of the things I like about you."

"Like your women pliable, do you?"

He laughed. "I like a lot of things about you, Ellie."

She twisted the sheet beneath her fingers. She liked a lot of things about him, too. Which was why she needed to end this conversation. "You said you wanted to give me some numbers."

He sighed. "Yeah, right. Got a pencil?"

She scrabbled in the drawer of the bedside table. "Fire away."

"These are private numbers. If you don't get me, then it will go to my voice mail. So you can call any time." He rattled off two numbers, one she recognized as his mobile phone.

"The Bellinghausens want to make sure they can always find you, don't they."

"Just call me Mr Indispensable."

She set the notepad on the nightstand. "I'd rather call you Joshua."

"Then do it. Goodnight, Ellie."

"Goodnight." She held the buzzing receiver in her hand. What in the world had that really been about? Was he feeling guilty over being so honest about not wanting a relationship? Maybe he'd expected her to suggest they get together again.

With all her heart, she wished she could. But there was no sense in playing in the ocean if you didn't know how to swim. She hung up the phone, feeling like she was severing a connection with him she had no business even thinking about.

The emptiness of the house pressed in, burrowed into her heart until a deep sense of desolation swept through her. Much as she loved her sisters, sometimes the future stretched out endlessly lonely. If her situation were different, would she be able to hold the interest of Joshua for very long? Unhappy with the answer, unable to keep her feelings in any longer, she turned out the light, hugged her pillow and cried until she was so exhausted, sleep claimed her.

Joshua rolled to his side, pulling the feather pillow against him. How he wished he were holding Ellie, stroking her soft skin, instead of thrashing in this cold bed with a prickly pillow. He tossed the pillow onto the floor and turned onto his back.

She'd call. If she'd had any uncertainty about doing so, his phone call should have reassured her.

If she was the type of woman he thought she was, she wouldn't be able to walk away from what they'd shared. Which was fine with him.

Ellie might not be marriage material, but that didn't mean they couldn't see each other again. Blanco wasn't far from home. There were weekends. Sometimes he was near there on business anyway. Or he could be if he wanted.

No, Ellie just wasn't what he pictured when he thought of taking a wife. He couldn't, however, imagine anyone else in the role either. Probably because this kind of thinking was still pretty foreign to a man who knew marriage as just a means to an end.

He'd watched his father get suckered in time after time with ideas of ever-lasting love. No way was he going to make the same mistake. Instead, he'd find a woman he could have a comfortable, safe arrangement with. Produce the required heir.

That would never work with Ellie. How could you have a comfortable arrangement with a woman who put you in such a fever your brains fried when you were with her? He loved to touch her, loved the way she'd touched him. That kind of stuff never lasted, though.

She hadn't given him any reason to think she'd see him again. Other than the soft look in her eyes when he'd kissed her goodbye. The way she'd kind of melted into him.

All good for a while, but not what you could

build a life time on. She was too stubborn, too secretive, too independent.

He wondered how long it would take her to call.

Sunday dragged.

Ellie couldn't remember ever having such a long, nothing kind of day. Jenna called and said she and Lauren would be home as soon as they could get a flight out, Monday or Tuesday. Tests completed, the doctors wanted to review several of them and then discuss their options. Since financing any surgery would require a major fund raising effort, they might just as well return to Blanco.

Ellie was glad she wouldn't be alone much longer. Being alone meant too much time to think about Joshua, an endeavor with no purpose to it. She graded papers and went to bed early, but sleep was a long time coming.

She returned to the farm late Monday afternoon after school. Jenna sat in the white wicker rocker on the long porch, but surprise at seeing her sister wasn't what made Ellie slam on the brakes and narrowly miss the trellis.

Dozens of flowers decked the porch. A profusion of pink carnations, dahlias, snapdragons and roses spilled across the worn wooden floor. Lauren skipped down the steps and raced to the truck before Ellie had even shut off the engine. Dazed, she climbed down from the cab.

"Oh, Ellie, isn't it exciting! And they're all for you. Can I have the yellow snapdragons to put in my room?"

"Of course, Buttercup. But don't run. You know it's not good for you." Ellie closed the door and slowly made her way to the house where Jenna had risen to stand leaning against the railing. She handed a card to Ellie.

Ellie glanced at the bold writing without seeing a word, then stared at the flowers. She didn't have to read the card to know who had sent them. Joshua must have bought out the local florist. How could he afford to?

The man was entirely too free with his money. Didn't he care how hard it was to come by? Talk about irresponsible. The huge wad of cash he carried around, the fancy car, the lavish hotel suite in Austin. It all added up to more than the average ranch foreman made.

"You should have been here when they were delivered. It kind of reminded me of that old circus trick where the clowns just keep piling out of a tiny car. Who is he, Ellie?"

"His name is Joshua. He's the man I met in Austin."

Jenna looked startled and anxiously searched her face. "Oh, no. How did he find you?"

"He works for the Bellinghausens. When Barrett came to argue about the bull again, he came with him." She read the card to avoid Jenna's dismayed expression. 'I didn't know what your favorite was, so got some of each. Enjoy. Joshua B.' As if she knew more than one Joshua who would send any flowers at all, let alone enough to decorate a hall for a wedding.

Lauren gathered up the bouquet of snapdragons. "Ellie's got a boyfriend," she sang.

Ellie pulled her close for a quick hug. "Hardly."

"Yes, you do. Only boyfriends send flowers." She walked carefully into the house, but the minute she was out of sight, her feet skipped up the stairs. Her childish chant drifted down. "Ellie's got a boyfriend; Ellie's got a boyfriend."

Jenna touched her arm. "What are you going to do?"

Ellie fingered a pink carnation. "Nothing." She sighed. She hadn't planned to share the details of her weekend, but now had no choice. "He said he didn't want the money back, he only wanted to see me again. I agreed to meet him in Austin last Friday night, then I came home. End of story."

Jenna shook her head. "I realize my dating experience is nearly as limited as yours, but trust me. No man sends flowers to a woman he doesn't plan to see again. And no man sends a hothouse full unless he's got an agenda."

"You're wrong. He's just a very extravagant man." She thought again of the Jaguar. The license read *Belle 1*. A company car, he'd said.

"Sure, and you're not interested in him at all."

"I'm not."

Jenna put her arms around her. "You can fool yourself as long as you want, Ellie Winfield, but you don't fool me." She released her and sat on the porch railing. "But we've got other problems."

"What did the doctors say?"

"They think she's got a real chance. If she has the surgery soon. If it works, it would be a permanent fix."

Ellie sank to the steps. "How much?"

"A lot more than we can hope to raise." Jenna's brown eyes filled with tears. "There's got to be a way to help her. But don't you dare do anything crazy again. I can't take worrying about both of you."

Guilt snaked through her. Here she'd been acting as if what she did had no impact on anyone else, and her sister was fretting about her. "I'm fine." Ellie patted her arm. "We'll find a way to help Lauren. No matter what it takes."

She rose and moved towards the door. Jenna sat down in the swing.

"Oh, I almost forgot. Taylor called. Wants you to call her at home tonight."

Ellie paused at the door. "She probably wants to go over the lab report with me. Hope she doesn't tell me my cholesterol is too high." Especially after all the ice cream she and Joshua had consumed Friday night.

She waited until after dinner and Lauren was

settled in bed before she called.

"Hi, Taylor. It's Ellie."

"You won't believe what happened. I have a new lab tech. Well, she's messed things up but good. I know it's hard for you to get back to Austin, but could you come by on Friday? We'll redo the tests, then how about you spending the night? It'll give us a chance to catch up."

"Sure. I can arrange that now that Jenna is back." A frisson of alarm raced through her. Was Taylor hiding something from her? For an instant, she had a vivid recollection of the first night she'd been with Joshua, the heat of his body curved around her backside, the smooth hard feel of him inside her.

No, they'd been careful. That last part was a dream, born of longing for what wasn't meant to be. "Anything I need to be concerned about?"

"No, but I'm considering looking for a new assistant. Don't worry, Ellie. Everything is fine. See you Friday."

She hung up the phone and met Jenna's concerned expression. "Taylor's new lab assistant messed up my blood work. I'll have to go back on Friday so they can redo it. She wants me to spend the night."

Jenna relaxed and patted her shoulder. "Good, you could use some time with friends. I can take care of things here."

The next day, Ellie stood in the teacher's lounge, staring at the piece of paper with Joshua's phone

numbers on it. She didn't want to call and give him
the impression she wanted to see him again, but not
acknowledging the flowers would be unbelievably
rude, even though she'd managed to convince
herself that a man who could shrug off two thousand
dollars wasn't going to make a big deal out of
sending flowers, even a porch full. To think he was
doing more than being generous and gracious served
no purpose at all. It wasn't as if he actually cared for
her.

The first number she dialed rang several times
before switching over to voice mail. She let herself
listen to the first part of his recorded message,
letting the warm-brandy sound of his voice seep
through her, then hung up without leaving a
message. If she didn't get him on the mobile
number, then she'd leave a message.

The phone rang twice before being picked up.

"Mama Belles, the dairy finest. How may I help
you?"

Startled by the sound of a woman's voice, Ellie
couldn't speak for several moments.

"Mr Bellinghausen's office. May I help you?"
The woman repeated.

Drat, somehow she'd reached Barrett's office.
She glanced at the sheet of paper again. No, this was
the number Joshua had given her. "I'd like to speak
with Joshua Bell, please."

The secretary hesitated a moment before
responding. "Mr Bellinghausen is in a meeting. May

I take a message?"

An awful buzzing started in her head, nearly drowning out the woman's repeated query. Ellie forced herself to ask one more time. "I need to leave a message for Joshua Bell, please."

"There is no Joshua Bell here, ma'am. However, if you'd like to leave a message for Joshua Bellinghausen," the woman stressed the last name, "I'll make sure he gets it."

She had to hang up before the dizziness made her collapse. "No. Thank you." She replaced the receiver and leaned against the wall.

It made an awful kind of sense. The cash, the Jaguar, Belle 1 on the license tag she'd watched in her rearview mirror all the way home from Austin. "Oh, me and Barrett go way back." Barrett must be his brother. She should have read that *Texas Monthly* article in Taylor's office. Then she'd know for sure. Mandy Sterns, the history teacher, had a subscription for her class.

Practically running, she hurried to Mandy's class, catching her about to enter the room. "Mandy, I need to borrow this month's issue of *Texas Monthly*."

Mandy gave her a puzzled look. "Looking for something to do on your break? That's a switch." She handed the magazine with Wilmer Bellinghausen's picture on the front cover to her.

"Isn't it something? A man gets a big spread in a magazine, then doesn't even get a chance to see it.

Let me know if you want to find out about those
yummy ice cream cowboys. My husband is one of
their route salesmen."

"Sure, Mandy. I want to dream about guys every
single woman in the state of Texas is scheming for."
She gave her friend a jaunty wave and hurried
outside.

Sitting on a bench near the main entrance, she
held the magazine in her hands for several moments,
staring at the cover picture. If this was Joshua's
father, he didn't look a bit like him. No wonder she
hadn't noticed it last Friday at Taylor's office.

Fingers shaking, she scanned the table of contents
and turned to the article written before Mr
Bellinghausen's death. She couldn't tear her
fascinated gaze from the pictures. Belle Ranch, a
fabulous spread thirty miles east of Austin. Mama
Belles, the Bellinghausen creamery. Pictures of
Barrett, who looked like a much younger version of
his father. Joshua, his black Stetson shading his face
into a combination of sex appeal and mystery that
made her heart constrict.

What a fool she was.

The feature article gave a history of the family
and the dairy. "End of a Dynasty?" proclaimed the
caption to a sidebar telling of Wilmer's untimely
demise. Ellie was transported back to the first night
she met Joshua. "You never told me what you're
celebrating."

"The death of a dynasty," he'd practically snarled at her.

Reading the article, she understood. Everything. His anger, the sense of loss that must have driven him to behave in such an unusual way. At last she realized why a man who could probably have any woman he wanted by simply crooking his finger, had taken a chance on a hooker. Her. Sex without complications.

Joshua and Barrett needed to marry and have children to claim their inheritance. For all she knew, he was engaged by now. All he'd wanted was a plaything. A diversion. Anger poured through her. For a while, she'd actually felt guilty about the money he'd spent on her. The whole thing was just pocket change to him.

She meant nothing.

Wasn't that what she'd wanted? Why did she feel so angry and gullible?

The warm spring air suddenly felt humid and stifling despite a light breeze. The cafeteria vegetable stew she'd eaten for lunch rumbled ominously in her stomach. A wave of queasiness washed through her. She took a deep breath and closed her eyes, trying to will the nausea away, but it was no use. She bolted inside, barely making it to the teacher's bathroom in time.

When she emerged, Mandy was seated in the lounge, eating a container of yogurt. "You're white as a ghost, Ellie. Something wrong?"

Ellie lay her head back on the cracked vinyl sofa and pressed a damp paper towel to her forehead. "Touch of flu, I guess."

Mandy nodded sympathetically. "Half of my class is out with it. Except in their cases I think it might be more in the nature of spring flu, if you get my drift."

Mandy shifted sideways on the couch. "Look, Ellie. I was talking to a few of the other teachers about Lauren. We all want to help."

"That's sweet, Mandy, but it's going to take a whole lot of money."

"That's just it." Mandy bounced a little, the motion sending a shiver of queasiness through Ellie. "We're going to have a booth at the Spring Fling to raise money. We'll sell raffle tickets, collect donations."

"Who besides our closest friends is just going to hand over cash?"

"Linda's husband is a travel agent. He's agreed to donate a trip and take care of the paperwork. All you have to do is say yes. We'll take care of everything else."

A weight lifted from Ellie. This could work. Tourist season was just starting. With the crush of outsiders who usually came to the arts and crafts fair in the small community in the Hill Country, they stood a good chance of raising some serious money, maybe even enough for Lauren to have her surgery as soon as school was out. Her elation lasted only a few moments as Mandy chattered excitedly and jolted the couch, sending another tremor of uneasiness through Ellie.

She didn't really believe she had the flu. Maybe it was the heat and the stress. Then another thought occurred to her.

Good God. What if she was seriously ill?

Joshua stared at his hand held phone as if it had somehow betrayed him. Why didn't the damn thing ring? Well, hell, she was a teacher. She probably couldn't get to a phone during the day but that didn't explain why she hadn't called last night. Perhaps he shouldn't have transferred his calls to his office, but one of the blasted ice cream machines had overflowed, and he couldn't afford to be interrupted while he tried to fix it.

Business always came first. What was the matter with him?

When he returned to his office, his secretary handed him a stack of messages. He quickly flipped through them. "No other calls?"

Ms Higgins looked at him over the top of her bifocals as if he were making a grievous error in thinking she might have neglected to pass along a message. "Those were the only ones who left messages."

Nearly to his office, he stopped. "Meaning?"

"A woman called. Wanting to reach a Joshua

Bell." Her slightly disapproving look made him feel
as if she could think of only one reason why a
woman would have his name wrong.

Ah, hell. Ellie. "So did she leave a message?"

The desperation in his voice must have softened
up the gray-haired matron who had been his father's
personal secretary for thirty years. She almost
smiled.

"I'm sorry, sir. If she calls again, I'll insist she
leave her name."

"Thanks." Joshua went in his office and closed
the door. Now what? Joshua Bell could have
accepted Ellie's phone call without qualms. For all
she knew he was just a ranch foreman.

Joshua Bellinghausen was another matter entirely.
If she called now that she knew who he really was,
he'd never be certain she wasn't as interested in the
money as most of the other red-blooded females in
Texas, especially considering the nature of their first
meeting.

Shit.

What had she needed the money for? Wondering
if DJ had overlooked something in his investigation,
Joshua tried to imagine Ellie buying expensive
clothes or jewelry, but it didn't fit. The dress she'd
worn the first night, although sexy, hadn't suited
either her personality or body well and must have
been borrowed. The clothes she'd worn last
weekend had been simple and singularly
unspectacular as was the outfit she'd worn the day

he and Barrett visited the farm.

So what had she done with the money?

The question continued to gnaw at him.

Tuesday night's dinner party was nearly as bad as Monday's. Gretchen had invited her two nieces over, and the poor women were as uninterested in him and Barrett as they were in them. And although he kept his portable phone with him, it remained dismayingly silent. Except for the call he got from the night-shift supervisor at the creamery.

His black mood darkened as the week wore on. Thursday night, after the guests left, he and Barrett sat in the study, sharing a gloomy silence.

Barrett sipped a whisky, neat. "I don't think I can take much more of this."

"You mean, guess who's coming for dinner next?"

"Not only that." He gestured with his glass. "You've been walking around for the past couple of days as if you've got barbed wire in your mouth. What the hell is the matter with you?"

Maybe talking it over with Barrett would enable him to put it into perspective. "Two words. Ellie Winfield."

Barrett chortled. "The Lone Star State's favorite bachelor has finally found a woman who can resist his dubious charms."

"Knock it off, will you? I've got a problem here."

"Let me guess. The lady's allergic to cut flowers."

Chagrined, Joshua scowled. "How did you know about that?"

"You left your credit card at the florist. I intercepted when they called the house. Which reminds me." He dug in his pocket and withdrew the plastic. "You might need this. Since you seem to be a bit short of cash these days."

"That's only because you're a welcher."

"One of these days, Joshua, you're going to get what's coming to you. I only hope I'll be there to see it happen." He grinned, taking the sting from his teasing. "Okay, so spill it. What's the big problem other than that you've forgotten how to dial a phone."

"Ellie called the creamery on Tuesday. At least I think she did. Well, Ms Higgins in her infinite efficiency, told her who I am."

"Ah, ha. Now you think that if she calls she's calling a Bellinghausen. Not simply getting in touch with Joshua."

"That's it."

"Why didn't you her tell her who you were?" He answered his own question. "Because when you met her in the first place she obviously needed money. So now you don't know what she wants from you, except you feel pretty sure it's not your sunshiny personality."

Joshua swirled the amber liquid in the brandy snifter. "Right again."

"What does DJ say about all this?"

"That Ellie gave up an offer of a big salary at some research institute in Boston ten years ago to go back to Blanco and teach school."

"Why?"

Joshua frowned. "DJ couldn't tell me." Which seemed odd, given how thorough he usually was. He probably didn't have the time to spend on a non-paying case, that was all, but he flatly refused to ever let Joshua pay him. He had a vague feeling his friend was holding out, but couldn't think of a reason why he'd do that. "Said I need to leave the lady alone and forget about it."

"Sounds like good advice." Barrett set his glass on the round table between the two wing back chairs. "Look, Joshua. You met this woman in a bar. She stole two grand from you and disappeared. You think she's from a good family, but that doesn't mean she doesn't have some really dark secrets. Leave it alone and forget about it."

Impossible.

He could manage to push thoughts of her from his mind while he was working, but at night he lay in bed wishing he were holding her. Hoping the phone would ring, he would then wonder what in hell he'd say if it did.

The note arrived in Friday's mail. "Dear Mr Bellinghausen." His name was underlined. "Thank you for the lovely flowers, but I must insist you honor our agreement. I'll return the money to you as soon as I am able. Ellie Winfield." He stared at the careful, round script. Anger simmered through his veins. He didn't want the money back, damn it. He wanted to see her again.

He showed the note to Barrett that night before the obligatory dinner with two more of the mommas' prospects. "So what do you think?"

Barrett fixed him a double bourbon. "I think she wants you to take a flying leap."

Genuinely shocked at his brother's comment, Joshua accepted the glass and took a gulp. "Why?"

"How should I know? Maybe she's the only woman you've ever met who doesn't think you're God's gift. Maybe she was simply conducting a scientific experiment."

That's what he was worried about. He'd replayed their first night together a hundred times and was still afraid he'd had one condom less than he'd needed. That couldn't have been her plan, though. She'd certainly been well prepared. He'd been determined to enjoy every minute of her. Very possibly he'd overdone it.

Not for the first time, he wondered if she hadn't expected to have sex with him at all. Maybe she had hoped to make off with the money with her virginity intact. The thought sobered him and caused no little amount of embarrassment. Had he misread her?

What had she needed the money for?

All of his other questions kept returning to that one.

"Let it go," Barrett advised, refilling his glass.

"The sooner you forget about this woman, the better you'll be able to take care of your real problem. Like how we're going to get the mommas off our backs."

"I wish it were that simple." Leaving the bourbon untouched, he headed for his room. The only solution was to see her again and insist she set the record straight. Then maybe he could put the whole puzzle of Ellie Winfield from his mind.

He stared at the phone for five minutes before finally picking it up and dialing Ellie's number. Hoping to hear her sweet voice, disappointment crashed over him at the sound of a child's voice.

"I'd like to speak to Ellie, please."

"She's gone all weekend. Who's this?"

Gone for the weekend? Remembering being the reason she was gone the weekend before made jealousy slam into him. Where had she gone? Who was she with this time?

He forced himself to take a deep breath. What the hell was wrong with him? He'd never felt this way before. "This is Joshua."

"You sent the flowers."

"That's right."

"Ellie let me have the snapdragons because yellow is my favorite color. Are you her boyfriend?"

Here was a way to get some information. Dismissing a twinge of guilt for taking advantage of the child, he decided to seize the opportunity.

"That's right. Who are you?"

"Lauren. I'm the little sister. Ellie never has boyfriends. When are you going to come see her?"

"Well, that's just it, Lauren. I wanted to see her this weekend, but I can't find the phone number for where she is staying."

"She went to see Dr Taylor. I don't know the number but Jenna does."

An ear-piercing yell came over the line as the child shouted for someone. In the background, he heard another feminine voice.

"Who are you talking to, Lauren?"

"Ellie's boyfriend." Again, the child's voice nearly split his eardrum. There was scuffling and hushed whispers, then the woman's voice came over the line.

"This is Jenna. Can I help you?"

"Hi, Jenna. This is Joshua." He hesitated. "Bellinghausen. I'm trying to reach Ellie. Can you give me a number where she can be reached?"

"I'm sorry, Mr Bellinghausen. I can't. She already told you she won't sell to you."

The line buzzed in his ear. She'd actually hung up on him! Then her words sank in.

Can't? Or wouldn't give him the number? Wait a minute. What did she mean, Ellie wouldn't sell to him?

Then another thought clobbered him. Who the hell was Dr Taylor?

Chapter Eight

Ellie sat on the deck of Taylor's contemporary home overlooking Lake Travis. "You have a gorgeous view, Taylor."

"It was a package deal. Came with the land." Taylor smiled and refilled Ellie's glass with sparkling apple juice.

Ellie gave her friend a quizzical look. When she and Taylor got together, they had been known to polish off a bottle of wine. Occasionally two. So what was with the apple juice? Taylor was edgy and nervous, unlike her usually cool, contained self.

"What gives?" A knot of dread grew in her stomach. Something terrible had shown up in her blood work. The nausea, the unrelenting weariness she'd felt for the past week were signs she was seriously ill. What if she had heart disease like she suspected was what had really claimed her mother? Or worse, although it was impossible to imagine anything more horrifying than dying during childbirth as her mother had.

Taylor sighed and clasped her hands together. "My patients always tell me what a terrific bedside manner I have, but I don't know how to say this, Ellie, so I'll just blurt it out. You're pregnant."

The bottom fell out of Ellie's world. She took a shaky sip of juice and forced a laugh. "That's not funny, Taylor."

"Because it's not a joke. Look, the reason I asked you to come back for another test was because I wanted to be absolutely certain after I examined you last week, but blood tests don't lie. You're four weeks along."

Ellie tried to set the glass down, but her hands were shaking so badly it toppled over and shattered on the glass table. "We were careful." Again the dream image raced through her mind. A dream. Surely, that time had been a dream.

Taylor held out her hands. "No method is 100%. You of all people should understand that."

She did, on an intellectual level, but emotionally she couldn't accept it. "You said your lab assistant made a mistake."

"So I lied. Knowing your situation, there was no way I was going to tell you this over the phone."

"I can't go through with this." But even as she said it, she knew it wasn't true. She could no more end the life than she could stop breathing. Even if the baby was as ill as she feared it might be, even if she had to endanger herself, she had to go through with it. She buried her face in her hands. What next?

Taylor put an arm around her shoulder. "I know you believe you have excellent reasons not to have children, Ellie, but won't you consider that maybe you've overstated the risk?"

She'd always believed any risk at all of not having a healthy child was too much. Knowingly subjecting an innocent life to what Lauren had gone through was not fair to the child. That was why she'd vowed never to take a chance on getting pregnant, why she'd known she couldn't ever get married. "How am I going to live with myself when there's a problem?"

Taylor gave her a gentle shake. "You don't know that there will be. I'll take super good care of you. We'll run tests when you're further along, just to make sure the baby is developing normally. Who is the father?"

Ellie dug the heels of her hands in her eyes and took a ragged breath. "You'll die when I tell you."

Taylor grinned. "Try me. I can't be shocked."

"Joshua Bellinghausen."

Taylor's jaw dropped. "I take that back. I think I just swallowed my teeth. *The* Joshua Bellinghausen? The ice-cream cowboy? Where on earth did you meet him?"

"At a hell hole in Austin." Ellie lifted her shoulders helplessly. "I didn't know who he really was at first." Or even the second time she'd been with him, but there was a limit to how much of the seamy story she wanted to share even with her best friend.

"I saw the article in *Texas Monthly*. I wouldn't mind checking out his flavor of the day myself," Taylor joked. "He's gorgeous, Ellie. And rich. And eligible. And he needs an heir. You're the perfect solution for him."

"Oh, no." Bad enough she was facing a pregnancy she hadn't wanted, she wasn't going to make a bad situation worse by taking a husband for all the wrong reasons.

"You have to tell him, Ellie."

She wondered if Taylor would think that if she knew the circumstances of what had brought them together in the first place. "We used condoms. They're usually pretty effective."

"Usually," Taylor agreed. "But it doesn't matter. You are most assuredly pregnant. You must have skipped a time."

"No," Ellie whispered, although now she was convinced that was what had happened. Dream indeed. How dare he?

"If you want me to help you tell him, I'd be glad to have both of you come to the office. Or here, if that makes it easier."

"If one can believe that article, he's got women hanging all over him. He's going to think I trapped him, when how could I have when I didn't even plan–" She couldn't exactly tell Taylor she'd just planned to take his money and run.

Taylor gripped her arm. "It doesn't matter if he thinks that at first. A lot of men do, initially. He'll get over it. And he has a right to know."

Telling him could mean having him involved in her life forever. Even though he definitely needed a more suitable wife than she could ever be, she couldn't picture him turning his back on his own child. Taylor was right, and no matter how hard Ellie tried to convince herself that her friend was wrong, she knew in her heart that somehow she'd have to find the courage to tell Joshua he was going to be a daddy.

Joshua brooded all weekend, two questions circling like vultures in his mind. Why had Ellie needed the money? Who was Dr Taylor? He considered calling DJ again and pushing him to find the answers, but since both he and Barrett thought he was off the deep end, he was reluctant to share his obsession any more than he already had.

Monday morning, Joshua toured the plant, checking out operations and wondered if he ought to take a drive to Austin and the communities west to call on some of the distributors himself. Usually he reserved that chore for the district manager, but the walls were closing in on him.

Maybe on Ellie's home turf, he'd be able to find some insight into the woman who now occupied an unhealthy amount of his thoughts.

He went to the break room for an ice cream bar as he always did in an effort to keep a finger on the pulse of employee attitudes, and the answer to his first question about Ellie slammed him between the eyes.

The colored poster on the break room wall caught
his attention, at first because company policy clearly
prohibited posting signs except on the employee
bulletin board. The second reason was because the
child pictured was the image of what Ellie must
have looked like twenty years ago. "Please help
Lauren," read the caption.

Lauren. The little girl who answered the phone at
Ellie's farm two nights ago? He wasn't aware of
how long he'd been scowling at the poster until one
of his drivers cleared his throat nervously and
repeated his name.

"Mr Bellinghausen? I guess I shouldn't have put
that up, but–" Carl twisted his cap in his hands.

Joshua brushed off his apology. "Local girl?"

"She lives about an hour west of Austin. Her
older sister teaches at Blanco High with my wife."
Carl edged towards the poster. "I'll just take that
down, sir."

"No, no." Joshua waved him away. "It's okay."
More than okay actually. He finally had the answer
to the question he'd tormented himself with for the
past four weeks. He stifled an impulse to throw his
arm around Carl shoulders. "How about if I call
your wife, Mandy isn't it? To see what the
Bellinghausens can do to help?"

Carl's face split into a grin. "Yes, sir."

"Got an extra poster?"

An hour later, Joshua sat in his office, the poster
in one hand, the phone in the other and made

arrangements with Mandy Stern for Mama Belles to supply ice cream for the fund raising booth Mandy was organizing at the Blanco Spring Fling. At least one person was delighted to get help. He wondered if Ellie would feel the same way.

Damn, she was secretive. Why hadn't she wanted to tell him about her sister? Did she really think he was heartless? Maybe considering the way they'd met and his insistence she "owed" him when he'd wanted to see her again, she had no reason to think anything else. If only he'd known, he would have been willing to give her anything she needed, not just because she so thoroughly captivated him, but because he'd never turn his back on someone who needed his help.

He let his brother in on the arrangements. Barrett agreed with his plan, but not with his reasons.

"I don't mind helping out someone in need, but if you're hoping to earn her gratitude, I don't think this will do it."

"I just want to help that little girl," Joshua insisted, not at all sure he didn't have ulterior motives. But hell, what difference did it make? He wanted to see Ellie again. Anything would do for an excuse. She was carrying one hell of a load of responsibility. No wonder she didn't have time to mess with a man who'd made it clear he didn't want any strings.

The day of the Spring Fling dawned clear and sunny. Joshua sat in his Jaguar across the street from the Blanco town square. Booths clustered around the perimeter of the sidewalk, bright awnings flapping in a light breeze. Although it was only nine o'clock, hundreds of people ambled through the square.

Here goes. The worst she could do was give him a chilly thank you. At least he'd be able to feel good about what he'd done, a feeling that had been somewhat lacking in his other encounters with Ellie, not counting the spectacular sex.

The thought that he'd pushed her into something she'd not really wanted continued to nag at him. Helping her sister was sure to allay the feeling. He found the teachers' booth next to one selling wood carvings. Unfortunately, Ellie was nowhere in sight.

A plump woman in her early forties, Mandy Sterns greeted him effusively.

"Mr Bellinghausen, how nice of you to come out here yourself. Let me introduce you to Lauren Winfield's sister."

Impossible hope flared in him even though he was certain Ellie hadn't yet made it to the fair. He turned and met the slightly hostile gaze of a short brunette, whose resemblance to Lauren wasn't nearly as striking as Ellie's was. Taking her hand, he studied her reaction.

No, she merely seemed curious about why he was there. Maybe she even thought he was donating the ice cream to earn her good favor in order to buy the bull. Ellie wouldn't have told her about who he was. Would she? "Nice to meet you, Jenna. Where is our poster girl?"

She had a firm handshake and a disturbingly direct gaze. "Home with our other sister, Ellie. We don't allow Lauren out among crowds, poor little thing." A slight frown marred her pretty face. "I know I've met your brother, but have we met before?"

Ah, hell. She might have been at Dandy Don's the night he met Ellie. He turned up the wattage on his smile, hoping to distract her enough to keep her from making the connection. "I don't believe so. Will you be here all day?" If so, he could dismiss any thought of seeing Ellie.

"No, just until noon. Ellie will be here after I go home to stay with Lauren."

Three hours. It seemed like a week away instead of merely 180 minutes. He settled in to wait, helping out as the day warmed and more people decided to sample the ice cream.

Noon came and went and still Jenna stayed. At quarter to one, she finally left.

He saw Ellie before anyone else in the booth caught sight of her. Her long hair gleamed golden in the spring sunshine, and his breath caught in his chest, squeezing his heart. Damn, but she was pretty, and totally unaware of it. Excusing himself to Mandy who was deep in conversation with another teacher, he made his way across the parking lot.

He wondered if luck would smile on him. Hopefully, he'd be able to get Ellie to take a break with him.

Her dress, a soft fabric print of pastel flowers, floated around her, enhancing her dainty femininity as she made her way through the crowd, then stopped at a booth of handmade jewelry.

Intent on examining a pair of delicately beaded earrings, Ellie didn't see him as she held the earrings up and admired them in a small mirror before she set them back down, a wistful look on her face. Suddenly he wanted to buy the entire collection of whatever the booth held, if she wished it. The feeling slammed headlong into him, stealing his breath as if he'd just run a marathon, startling him with the intensity. Just for the pleasure of watching her smile, he would give this woman anything.

Except the opportunity to say no.

He moved toward her, and she turned unexpectedly, bumping into him. Joshua reached out and steadied her. "I've been waiting for you."

Her breath came out in a little gasp. For a minute, her eyes reflected a flicker of pleasure and panic, then the determination he admired was back in place. "I brought lunch."

"Then I'm afraid you'll have to enjoy it alone. I have to help at one of the booths."

"No, you don't." He gently took her arm and
started leading her across the street toward where
the Jaguar sat. "I came to talk to you, and I'm not
going to leave until I do. Now you can go over to
the park with me where we can have some privacy,
or we can continue this discussion in front of a
couple of thousand curious onlookers."

Ellie craned her neck towards the booth and the
long line snaking out from it. "Why are so many
people there?"

"Most folks like ice cream on a warm spring
day."

She gasped, but tilted her chin at a stubborn
angle. "What did you do?"

"Nothing any other community minded
businessman wouldn't have if given the opportunity.
Bellinghausens donated the ice cream. Your friends
are selling it for a buck a scoop and making a haul
on the raffle tickets at the same time."

Ellie's eyes softened for a moment, again hitting
him square in the chest, then her gaze hardened to
blue-green chips. "That's very generous, and we
really appreciate it, but I don't believe we have
anything to talk about."

"I disagree." Damn, she was stubborn, and she
wasn't the least bit impressed by him. He liked that
about her. "Have you eaten lunch?"

She reluctantly shook her head. "No, but–"

"Great, because I brought something special."

She let him lead her to the car, but was silent on

the short drive. At the park, Joshua picked a spot near the river with a view of the small waterfall. He spread a blanket in the shade of a towering live oak, then set out the fixings in the gourmet basket he'd picked up on his way through Austin.

He handed her a glass of sparkling wine. Ellie eyed it doubtfully.

"It may not be your favorite vintage, but it's pretty good. Local stuff. From that winery in Llano."

"This is fine," she murmured, setting the glass down without even taking a sip.

Joshua chatted casually about the weather, the teahouse that had been a favorite of his father's and how he had visited Blanco a few times but had never run into her there. Although Ellie initially picked at a chicken salad sandwich, she finally finished hers and half of the extra one.

"Seems funny our paths never crossed."

"That's because you've never visited the high school. I don't hang around in town. As soon as classes are over, I go home."

"To be with Lauren?"

Her gaze flew to his. What was he after? "And Jenna. My sisters," she said carefully. "Then I have my research to work on in the evenings."

"And helping home school your sister, and taking care of the stock." He shook his head. "Who takes care of Ellie?"

She straightened. "I don't need anyone to take care of me, thank you."

"Everyone does." He reached up and rubbed a wavy strand of her hair between his fingers. "Why didn't you tell me about your little sister?"

"Why should I have? We don't know each other very well."

"I'd say we're intimately acquainted."

Her face flaming, Ellie started to say something, then snapped her mouth shut.

"Lauren is the reason you needed the money?"

"That's none of your business!"

"Like hell it's not. I've been racking my brain trying to understand what drove you to spend the night with me because I knew that once I had the answer, I'd know what kind of person you really are."

"And what have you decided, Mr Pinkerton? That I'm more or less honest than you are? At least I didn't give you a false name."

He rubbed his chin. "I apologize. I wasn't quite myself that night. And after that, I was angry for a while, then that damn article came out in *Texas Monthly*. You wouldn't believe what Barrett and I have to put up with."

"Poor thing."

"I want to help."

There it was, the pity she abhorred. He was only here now because he felt sorry for Lauren, not because there was a shred of feeling for her in his black heart.

She knew what he really wanted: someone to play with while he searched for a wife who could produce the required heir.

And she was supposed to tell this man she carried his baby? Ha! "And what do you want from me in exchange?"

"Jeez, what is with you? You think everything has a price tag?"

"Doesn't it?"

He pulled up a long stalk of grass and rolled it between his fingers. "It's not like I made any promises to you, Ellie."

"So what? I never said I wanted to see you again. What's the point? I vowed years ago that I would never get married. And if you don't want anything now, then you will later. I don't care who you are, Joshua Bellinghausen, I did what I had to, but I will not be a rich man's plaything."

"That's not why I'm here, damn it." His words emerged as a growl.

"Oh, really?"

"Ellie," his gaze searched her face.

She took a deep breath and clasped her hands together. "Don't you understand what you're doing to me? Although I deeply appreciate your generosity to my sister, I can't help but wonder what you expect to get from all this. I have nothing more to give you."

"I just want to spend some time with you."

"Why? You can't sit there and tell me you'd ever want anything long-term, can you? Not that I'd want you to." She held up her hands to make sure he got the point.

"True." He sighed. "It's not you, sugar. I can't picture myself married at all."

The honesty in his eyes took her by surprise but made her no less angry. Why did it bother her so much? Lunch turned to a sodden lump in her stomach. "So what does that leave? We sure can't be friends after what we've done together. What kind of person do you think I am, anyway?"

His eyes narrowed. "I thought you were the most giving, unselfish person I ever met, but I guess I was wrong. You're selfish as the day is long, Ellie Winfield."

She gasped. "How can you say that? I've given up my life for my sister."

"Yeah, but you're hell bent on showing the world that you don't need anyone, aren't you? You sold yourself for your sister, but you can't stand it if someone tries to do something for you. Well, in my book that makes you pretty damn selfish."

His words stung. How dare he say that to her! After all she'd done, after all she'd given up. "I already owe you two thousand dollars, Joshua, and now you've given away who knows how much today. There is no way I can ever repay you." The shame over what she'd done returned, and with it the horrible feeling she could never be free of obligations to him.

"I don't want the money, damn it." He wadded up the stalk of grass and threw it down on the blanket.

"That's only because you can't appreciate how hard it is to come by."

"Maybe not. I spent ten years on my own, scraping along, but it was definitely because I wanted to. I always had the option of going home. You were plumb out of choices, weren't you? That's what drove you to do what you did."

"I..." He couldn't know all of it, her father's abandonment of Lauren before she was even born. Her mother's shocking death. Lauren's continuing need for medical care that had bankrupt the farm. Ellie's constant struggle for her sisters and herself just to have a place to live and to have enough to eat. The weight of worries overwhelmed her, and her stomach rebelled.

Ellie closed her eyes. Oh, no. What was the matter with her? Morning sickness was supposed to be in the morning, not in the afternoon.

Please, God. Not now. She couldn't afford to disgrace herself in front of Joshua.

"Ellie. Ellie, what's wrong. You're practically turning green."

"Chicken salad," she mumbled and lurched to her feet, desperate to get away. She ran towards the stand of cypress trees along the river. He was behind her in an instant but by the time she reached the trees, she was too sick to care.

She wrapped her arms around her waist, trying to hold the nausea in, but it was no use. To make her humiliation complete, he held her hair back, then dabbed her mouth with a soft, monogrammed handkerchief when she was finished. Ellie leaned against a tree, tears streaking down her face, despite her efforts to control the wild emotions swinging through her.

"Ellie, honey. What is going on? Why are you crying?"

She took a shuddering breath. "I'm pregnant, damn you."

He reached out a gentle hand and touched her shoulder. "Wow." His voice contained a mixture of apprehension and awe.

"I didn't want this to happen!"

"I know, I know," he said quietly. "It's my fault."

"No kidding!" She turned to face him, wiping away tears with the back of her hand. "I just don't understand how, when we were so careful every time."

He rubbed a hand over his face. "Well, now, that's not entirely true. That first night. I guess the condoms were depleted before I was. Remember?"

"Oh," she gasped. So it hadn't been a dream. She just stared at him for several moments. Here she'd thought they were victims of bad luck, and he'd known all along what kind of chance they'd taken. That was why he'd given her his private phone numbers, to make sure she could find him. Too bad he hadn't seen fit to let her know the reason why he wanted to stay in touch had nothing to do with wanting to see her because he had a shred of feeling for her.

She flew into him, fists pummeling his chest. He stood there, solid as a pillar and let her vent her anger. "How could you? Don't you know what you've done?"

"Obviously I wasn't thinking clearly."

"I'll say." His unruffled acceptance infuriated her. Didn't he understand the magnitude of their dilemma? "I suppose you think you can just throw some money at this problem and it will go away." She thumped him on the chest again, although much of the heat of her anger had already dissipated. *"I hate you."*

"No, you don't." His calm conviction annoyed her even more when he put his arms around her.

"Yes, I do." She wrapped her arms around his waist and buried her face against his shirt. "I never wanted this."

"I know." He rubbed his hands down her back, patting, trying to soothe. A baby. A tiny bit of elation crept past his initial misgivings. He'd spent the past four weeks trying to convince himself he didn't want a relationship with Ellie Winfield. He'd listed dozens of reasons why she wasn't a good choice for a wife, but in one instant all the reasons why not had coalesced into the only positive reason that mattered.

His baby. Ellie was pregnant with his baby. "We're getting married."

"No, we're not."

"Oh, yes we are."

"You just finished telling me you're not the marrying kind."

"So I changed my mind."

"Everyone will say I trapped you."

"Probably." Meaning it as a joke, he wasn't prepared for a fresh onslaught of her tears. "Ellie, honey, I was kidding." He knew she hadn't trapped him, but wasn't sure at all that he hadn't trapped her.

What had possessed him? But he knew. The warm sweetness of her. The feeling of wholeness he only had when he was with her. Not that the reasons mattered. They were getting married, and that was that.

Snatching his handkerchief and stepping back from him, Ellie dried her tears. "I will not marry you, you arrogant–" she sputtered.

"Yes, you will. We're going to do it right, too." He held his hands out, as if giving closing arguments to a case before a jury. "Big wedding. You choose where. I'll pay for it."

"I'll do no such thing."

"Then I'll choose. I have as much right to that baby as you do. More, if you consider that it's my fault. Everyone in the Hill Country, hell, in the state is going to know that's my baby, Ellie. You better get used to the idea of being married, because you can't afford to have people in this little town finding out how you and I got together in the first place."

Ellie looked aghast. "Are you blackmailing me?"

"If that's what it takes."

"A marriage of convenience, then."

He knew what she meant, and the idea of her sharing his name and not his bed filled him with dismay, then determination that there was no way that would happen. "Now wait a minute,"

"You don't love me."

He detected the slightest bit of wistfulness in her voice, but she stood proudly away from him, her arms crossed.

"Sugar, I watched my father get married five times after my mother died. I'm not sure I know what love is." Relieved when she didn't move back when he stepped closer, he cupped her face in his hands. "I may not be a prize in the romance department, but I swear I'll be good to you. And our child will never want for anything."

To his surprise, his words unleashed another torrent of tears. He pulled her into his arms and mentally backpedaled as fast as he could. What had he said? "I didn't mean to sound so cold. Ellie, I haven't been able to stop thinking about you since the day we met. And I know you like me, at least a little. We can make this work, I know we can."

"I do like you, Joshua." Her whispered words

were barely audible. "I'm just so scared. The baby—"

"Hush." He stroked her hair, pressed her closer as if that might take away the anxiety he could feel trembling in her small body. "It's going to be okay. A lot of people get started with a helluva lot less."

Maybe in time, she'd realize that even if he could never tell her he loved her, she held one hundred percent of his commitment. Hopefully, that would be enough.

"I can't do this."

He tensed. What did she mean? She wouldn't. . . . Thinking she might not want to go through with the pregnancy alarmed him. Suddenly, having Ellie be his wife and bear his child was more important than anything else that could happen in his life.

"I can't marry you, Joshua."

Her words filled him first with surprise, then with determination. She gripped the front of his shirt so tightly, he was amazed the fabric didn't shred beneath her fingers.

"I never intended to have children. After what happened to my mother—After what we've been through with Lauren—If there's something wrong with our baby, how will you live with the idea of knowing it would be your only one?"

He let out a breath. Our baby. She wouldn't say that if she didn't intend to go through with the pregnancy. He didn't understand how something he hadn't known about thirty minutes ago could have grabbed a hold of him so thoroughly, but the need to take care of his own consumed him. First he had to convince Ellie, though. "Odds are in our favor. You have to know that."

"But, Joshua–"

"We're getting married, Ellie, and that's final."

Chapter Nine

For the first time in years, Ellie let someone else do the planning. Joshua Bellinghausen might not love her, but he knew how to make things happen. By the time they reached the fair, she felt calmer listening to him outline his plan.

"This is the perfect place for people to see us together. We'll go to Austin next weekend, pick out a ring, then stay at Belle Ranch so you can meet the rest of my family. We can announce our engagement a week or so later."

"I've already met Barrett. Who else is there?"

Joshua gave her a rueful grin. "Five ladies who are going to be thrilled to pieces to meet you."

He couldn't mean his father's ex-wives. Certainly, they wouldn't all still live at the ranch. Too overwhelmed to contemplate it, Ellie let herself be carried along in his planning.

"I'll be at your farm Friday night to pick you up."

"Joshua, I can certainly drive to Elgin myself."

He looked doubtful. "That old truck doesn't look as if it will get as far as the feed store. Besides, I'd like you all to myself for a while so we can get our story straight, especially since we can't exactly share a bedroom at the ranch."

The thought was oddly disappointing, but she was touched that he had such regard for keeping up appearances to his family.

He touched her hand. "You sure you feel good enough to stay here the rest of the afternoon?"

She gave him a weak smile. "I could use a nap, but I'll be okay."

He frowned and was silent for a few moments. "I'll drive home with you after the fair and help you explain things to your sister."

He certainly was a bulldozer when he made up his mind to do something. "That's not necessary. How will you get home if you leave your car here?"

He grinned. "I'll bet I can work around it. Does Jenna know you're pregnant?"

Ellie shook her head and blinked back tears. How was she going to tell Jenna? Her older sister was the only one who could fully appreciate Ellie's fears about the baby. How was she going to react to the pregnancy, let alone a marriage that would leave her alone, assuming Joshua would let Lauren come live with them.

She closed her eyes and rested her head against the seat back. Maybe it would be better if Joshua were there, too. That way, at least Jenna would be reassured about what kind of man he was. Who knows? Maybe it would alleviate her own doubts.

He held her hand as they made their way through the crowd in the town square. In his black jeans, crisp Western shirt with the sleeves rolled up to expose strong forearms, and a black Stetson tipped back on his head, he cut a figure that had everyone staring and whispering behind their hands. Ellie was half embarrassed, half pleased when he unexpectedly dropped a light kiss against her mouth just as they reached the booth.

"I always did want to kiss a pretty girl in front of everyone," he whispered.

Ellie looked up and saw Mandy break into a delighted grin. "You're going to ruin my reputation."

"Not since you're letting me make an honest woman out of you," he murmured. He winked, smiled, then he was turning on the charm to Ellie's dazzled co-workers.

Ellie took her place in the booth and watched the bevy of whispering, giggling girls in line behind brash teenage boys. Half of her class stood before her, looking expectantly at her as if certain that plain, boring Miss Winfield would share with them who the handsome cowboy was.

Mandy squeezed her arm. "Why didn't you tell me you knew Joshua Bellinghausen, Ellie?"

"Why didn't you tell me he'd donated the ice cream," she countered.

"He asked me not to." Mandy's eyes grew wide. "Oh, I get it. He wanted to surprise you." She lowered her voice. "Is there something going on between you two?"

"I'll keep you posted, Mandy," she said, knowing

that by noon on Monday everyone at Blanco High would know that Ellie and Joshua had a thing going on. Joshua was right: she couldn't afford the scandal her pregnancy would cause. Not only for herself, but also because of her sisters.

Marriage to him was the only way to escape that. But she couldn't help but think she was trading a bad situation for a worse one.

Jenna did not take the news well. Eyes flashing sparks, it was obvious that she didn't think much of Joshua Bellinghausen. Just as obvious that she would as soon offer him the business end of Granddad's Winchester as the coffee and the apple turnovers she and Lauren had baked that afternoon.

Lauren, however, was thrilled, whether at the prospect of being a junior bridesmaid or because of the four-foot teddy bear and the triple chocolate ice cream Joshua brought her was hard to tell. Chattering excitedly, she followed Jenna to the kitchen when she left to replenish the coffeepot. Her voice drifted back to the living room.

"I told you so. Ellie did too have a boyfriend. I think he's nice, Jenna, don't you?"

Thankfully, Jenna's answer was indistinct. Ellie sank back into the chintz cushions of the sofa and closed her eyes.

Joshua took her hand and gently stroked her fingers. "You look beat. I think I'll shove off so you can get some rest and let things settle down here. Are you going to be okay?"

"Sure." She watched him pick up his hat and wished she had the courage to ask for a hug.

"You have a very expressive face, you know?" He plopped back down on the couch and gathered her close, caressing her back and rubbing his cheek against her hair. "But it would help if you quit being so skittish about telling me what you want."

Having been the one everyone in the family turned to for so long, she wasn't sure she could. She burrowed against him, letting his solid warmth wrap around her. Maybe he wouldn't ever love her. Maybe this was the last thing she had ever expected to happen. Maybe this baby would be okay, but there was no way she'd take a chance again.

"I meant what I said, Joshua. I won't do this more than once."

"Get married? I hope not." His chuckle rumbled beneath her ear.

Ellie plucked at a button on his shirt. "The baby." She sat up and searched his face. "If we're getting married, you need to be convinced of that. I won't have more than this one."

"It's not *if,* darlin', it's *since*. And I think you're getting a little ahead of us both."

She had to make sure he understood, even if she couldn't share all the reasons why just yet. The pregnancy was still too new, her emotions too raw to explain everything. "I just want to make sure you understand my feelings about this."

"I understand your concern, I truly do, but I still think you might be overstating things." He pulled her against him again and continued to massage her back. "Who's your doctor? Someone here?"

"My roommate from college. Taylor Hunnicutt. She has an ob-gyn practice in Austin."

"Is that why you went to Austin two weeks ago, why you were able to meet me there?"

"Umm."

"Is that when you found out?"

Uh oh. Even though his voice was calm, his body was as tense as a coiled spring. "No, I found out a week ago."

He relaxed slightly. "It bothers me a little wondering how long you planned to wait to tell me, Ellie, but I guess that doesn't matter now." He placed a finger under her chin and tilted her face up to meet his gaze. "Not being the kind of man who's afraid of my responsibilities, I expect you to keep me in the information loop every step of the way. Next time you go to the doctor, I'm going with you."

"You don't have to do that."

"You never give up, do you? I'm a part of this, whether you like it or not." He sighed, gave her a hug that nearly cracked her ribs, then rose. "I'll call you tomorrow."

The door banged behind him, leaving the house barren without his overpowering presence. Ellie looked up to see Jenna standing in the doorway holding the thermal carafe of coffee. Her expression was tight.

"Does he know the kind of risk you're taking?"

Ellie plucked at a loose thread on the couch, her sister's fear striking her all the way to her heart. She'd tried to tell him, but had she tried hard enough? "Not completely. I don't think he believes that I know what I'm talking about." She sighed. "What difference does it make now? I can't turn the clock back."

Jenna sank to the couch. "I feel like this is all my fault."

Ellie whipped a startled gaze to her sister. "Your fault? How do you figure that? You did your best to talk me out of going there that night."

"I should have tried harder. Do you really think marrying him is the answer?"

She laughed ruefully. "It's the only one he'd accept." She spread her hands. "You've got to admit he's not likely to turn his back on his own child. Not like our father did." At least she hoped not. With all her heart, she hoped Joshua wouldn't turn out to be the kind of man who'd abandon his family when they needed him the most. "This isn't just about me, unfortunately. If anyone in town found out what I did, none of us would be able to hold our heads up. I can't do that to you. Or Lauren, especially. She needs all the support we can find for her. Plus I'd probably lose my job."

"Whereas this way, you get to quit. What a choice." Jenna squeezed her hands. "Why is he so set on having a big wedding?"

"He thinks people will speculate less. If it was up to me, we'd sneak off to Vegas and maintain separate households."

Jenna rolled her eyes. "That would really look good." She hugged herself. "You're certainly going to be the envy of a lot of other women. I just hope you don't end up with the heartache that usually goes along with that."

Joshua's sense of well being increased steadily as he neared Belle Ranch. Perhaps it wasn't the best set of circumstances, but Ellie had certainly solved his two worst problems: finding a wife and starting a family, and a chance to ease the gnawing sense of dissatisfied loneliness he felt every night when he went to bed. He couldn't wait until she moved to the ranch.

He snared Barrett and ushered him into the study as soon as he got home. "Who's on the menu tonight?"

"Rosemary's about run through the local stock. Unfortunately, Monica's convinced we'll be happier with her hand picked debutantes."

Handing his brother a bourbon and fixing one for himself, Joshua pondered the best way to share his news. "Finally figured out a way to get the

Winfields to turn that bull over to you."

"What? Marry Ellie?" Barrett took a healthy swig of his drink.

"Yup. I'd sure like you to be best man."

Barrett sputtered through a mouthful of bourbon. "I was joking, for pete's sake."

"I'm not."

"Come on, Joshua. Think about this."

"I have. Plenty. Marrying Ellie is the answer to a lot of things."

"Oh, I get it. She told you she's pregnant, like that isn't the oldest trick in the book."

For a moment, Barrett's words made his hackles rise. Subduing his temper with an effort, Joshua chose his next words carefully. After all, Barrett only had his interests at heart. "Right again. But actually, I had a tough time convincing her we should get married."

"Well, at least one of you is being reasonable. I agree you have a responsibility to her, Joshua, but marriage? You barely know her!"

He knew as much as he needed to. The deep loyalty and obligation she had towards her family awed him. He wondered if he would have the courage to do the same kind of thing and although he knew he'd lay his life down for his brother, he wasn't sure about the answer. No, there was no doubt that Ellie would stay for the long haul. He certainly wasn't about to play musical wives as his father had done.

"Well, that's the way it's going to be. I wanted you to be the first to know."

"I suppose her family is thrilled."

"Hardly." Joshua grimaced. "I thought Jenna Winfield was going to take a gun to me." He finished off his drink. "Let's get dinner over with. I'd just as soon wait till this weekend to break the good news to the mommas."

After dinner, he escaped to his room, using a vague comment about work as an excuse to avoid the desultory discussion Monica insisted on having about who was going to be invited to dinner next. Not to mention her sulks when Joshua had put his foot down about having any more company for a while.

He prowled around, polishing his boots, reading the ranch reports Barrett had given him, but the telephone lured him time and again. Ellie was probably sleeping. He'd said he'd call her tomorrow.

But the need to hear her voice again proved too strong. She answered on the first ring. Obviously, she wasn't ready to sleep any more than he was.

"Hey, Ellie. It's Joshua."

"Hey, yourself."

Her sweet voice sent a rush of desire racing through him. "You never told me your favorite flavor."

She hesitated, and he imagined all the things he wanted her to tell him. Like how she missed him.

How she wanted him to make love to her all night
long. He sighed. "Ice cream. I want to send you
some."

"Surprise me."

He planned to do just that. Despite what he'd told
her about not sharing a room at the ranch when she
visited this weekend, he wasn't about to have her
under the same roof and not under the same covers.
"I will. Did your sister settle down?"

"Yeah, she's coming around. I'm just tired."

"How's Junior?"

"Okay, I guess."

Her voice held a little hitch that caught him off
guard, made him wish he could again gather her
close and hold her until her fears disappeared.
Surprised at how the sound of her voice made the
loneliness of his room multiply ten times, he wanted
to tell her how much he missed being with her, but
the words stuck in his throat. "Well, I'll say
goodnight then."

"Good night, Joshua." He held the receiver long
after the line buzzed in his ear. What the hell was
the matter with him? He was in essence planning a
merger for what amounted to business reasons, and
he was staring at the phone like a calf that'd gotten a
belly full of bad hay.

Ellie turned off the light and burrowed under the
comforter as if that would somehow ease the ache

that had taken hold of her heart. Why had he called when he'd said he'd call tomorrow? She supposed that meant she wouldn't hear from him for a few days. Maybe not even until he came to pick her up on Friday.

How's Junior? There was no mistaking the possessiveness in his voice. Not that it meant anything. If she wasn't careful, he'd soon have her convinced he owned her, the way he was in control of everything at Belle Ranch.

She thought of the pictures in the magazine. It was a magnificent ranch. Ellison Farms looked like a garden patch in comparison. What on earth would she be expected to do there? If Joshua would see to it that she could continue her research, she and Barrett could work with the bull he'd wanted. Maybe that would allow her to feel as if she were contributing something to the marriage besides problems.

She smoothed a hand over her flat stomach, trying to picture what she knew was going to happen and whispered a prayer that everything would work out for the best. "Oh, baby," she murmured. "What have I gotten us into?"

Joshua called every night, surprising Ellie when the phone rang shortly after she got into bed. She could write the script for each call. He'd ask how she was, then about the baby, then tell her he'd see her on Friday, perhaps so she wouldn't be expecting to hear from him again. But she always did.

Friday afternoon, Joshua was waiting at Ellison Farms when she walked up the lane from the highway where the school bus dropped her off. Ellie approached the porch where Joshua sat visiting with Lauren. Or actually Lauren was chattering away as fast as a car on the Indy 500, and Joshua was doing an excellent job of appearing engrossed in hearing about her dreams to someday be a world famous race car driver.

Jenna was right: she was going to be the envy of a lot of women. In black jeans and a green and black plaid shirt that made his eyes look even greener, he looked charming and at ease on the weathered porch. Ellie's heart made a funny little flip.

Stop it. He was taking care of his responsibilities, nothing more. She'd often heard it said that in every relationship one person cared more than the other did. She couldn't afford to let it be her.

She was silent for a long time after they left the farm, staring out the window, watching the budding green in the fields roll past. Bluebonnets and Indian paintbrush splashed the roadside with bright colors. She definitely was not looking forward to this weekend, meeting his family, then the trip to Austin to get a ring she didn't want.

Now, if the situation were different, she could picture the fun of trying on diamonds, maybe a sapphire with a couple of small diamonds alongside.

She sighed. Better to keep it simple. She'd bet
anything Joshua was the plain gold band type.

"What are you thinking about that's got you
looking like you bit into a prickly pear?" His voice
broke into her troubled thoughts.

"Just wondering what your family thinks."

"Nothing yet. Except for Barrett, I haven't told
anyone."

Aghast, Ellie shifted in the leather bucket seat.
"Please tell me you're kidding. I'm about to be
dropped into the midst of people who don't have a
clue about what's going on?"

He spread his hands over the steering wheel. "It'll
be fine. Believe me, they're going to love you."

Again, he didn't seem eager to tell her just who
"they" were. "How did Barrett take it?"

"Oh, he was surprised, but he understands."

Ellie sank into her seat. Great. "He knows we're
getting married because I'm pregnant, right?"

"Ellie, I can't avoid telling my brother what the
situation is."

"Does he also know how we met?"

This time Joshua shifted uncomfortably. "Sort of.
He knows you took my money. He doesn't know we
had agreed you take some of it. I felt like that was
better."

Ellie threw up her hands. "Oh, yes. Much better
he thinks I'm a thief than a hooker."

"Especially since you're not."

"I was for one night, wasn't I?"

He shot her an annoyed glance. "I don't think that counts."

"And why not?"

"Well, for one thing, I think we can write it off as just a different way of two people getting together. For another, I don't think you had really intended to go through with it." The silence stretched between them. "Am I right?"

Ellie stared at her hands, clenched tightly in her lap. "You're right. I was hoping I wouldn't have to."

"But you did. And for damn good reasons."

"I would do anything for my family." Her voice low, she shot him a defiant look, expecting him to tell her there were limits to which decent people would go, even for the people they loved. To her surprise, he reached over and took her hand, wrapping his fingers around hers. A spark of admiration lit his eyes.

"I know, darlin'. That's why I think we can make this work."

The last rays of setting sun streaked Belle Ranch with glorious pinks and purples and cast the white pillars of the mansion with soft pastels. A long paved drive wound over a small stream, then rose to the higher ground the house resided on.

A wild profusion of border plants circled the walk and grew thickly beneath flowering crepe myrtle.

Indian hawthorne and pink azaleas clustered near
the house. Ellie's breath caught in her throat. The
pictures in *Texas Monthly* hadn't done it justice.

"Oh, Joshua. What a beautiful place."

"Esther's quite a gardener." Joshua pulled her
small suitcase from the trunk of the Jaguar.

"Who is Esther?"

A grin tugged the corner of his mouth. "You'll
see."

Ellie followed him up the walk. Who were these
people he kept referring to? The house staff
perhaps? Certainly, an enormous house with
grounds like this required a great many people to
work on it. Did he plan on having her meet them all
this weekend?

The oak front door swung wide before she'd
taken her first step onto the porch. Sparkling light
spilled out as a feminine voice greeted Joshua
enthusiastically.

"Is this your surprise? Joshua, she's darling!"

Ellie found herself swept inside the house, both
her hands clasped by a very motherly looking
woman dressed in a flower print dress.

"I'm Rosemary, dear. We had no idea, did we
girls?"

Standing behind her were four other women
ranging in age from Rosemary's late fifties to one
who looked close to Joshua's age, all eyeing Ellie
with undisguised interest. Panic edged up. Who
were these people?

Joshua set the suitcase aside and sighed, but amusement filled his expression. He knew she was worried, and he thought it was funny! She tilted her chin and assumed a confident air but wished he'd take her hand, as if they actually were a blissfully happy couple, announcing their engagement.

"Mothers, this is Ellie Winfield. My fiancée."

Happy or not, there was no mistaking a hint of possessiveness in his voice, or was that just wishful thinking on her part?

"Ellie, these are my step-mothers, Rosemary, Gretchen, Belinda, Esther, and Monica."

Although they smiled, each woman looked as if they wanted their turn to interview her for the job of Joshua's wife. What was she going to say to them?

Ellie took a tiny step back and came up against his solid body. How she wished he'd touch her and make her feel more like she really was supposed to be here.

Most new brides had all they could do pleasing one mother-in-law. Lucky her. She was going to have five.

Chapter Ten

Joshua couldn't stop himself from cupping his hands on her shoulders and savoring the closeness of her. Ellie shot him a startled look over her shoulder. Man, she was nervous. What did she think was going to happen? He leaned down to whisper in her ear. "Relax. They're not going to bite you."

Barrett, his expression barely cordial, emerged from the drawing room, a glass of bourbon in hand.

"Barrett might, though. So I'd give him a wide berth."

His brother scowled. "What kind of stories are you telling her?"

Joshua let his hand trail down Ellie's bare arm before lacing his fingers with hers. "Just telling her what a nice guy you are."

"Hi, Barrett. We met at the farm a couple of weeks ago." Ellie's voice was gentle, but strong.

He nodded, his expression softening slightly. "You look different without your glasses."

Ellie blushed, the color slowly creeping from her pretty face down her neck. Joshua bit back a laugh. Luckily, Rosemary kicked into her gracious Southern lady hostess mode.

"Here we stand chattering in the hallway. Please,

Ellie. Come in. We were just enjoying a cocktail before dinner. Barrett will fix you one."

"She doesn't want—" Joshua began, then Ellie's elbow caught him none too gently in the ribs.

"I'd love some orange juice, if you have it. Or a ginger ale."

Barrett started to grin. "Sure. Orange juice it is."

Ellie preceded them into the parlor, the picture of grace and charm in a yellow flowered dress that flowed past her knees. Barrett leaned towards Joshua.

"Not going to lead this one around, are you?" He chuckled. "This might be okay, after all."

Somehow Ellie made it through dinner and the challenge of listening patiently to five women give their opinions on just exactly what she and Joshua needed to have the perfect wedding.

Luckily, Joshua saw how tired she was and insisted on escorting her to her room as soon as the meal was over. Large and airy, the bedroom suite located on the back of the house with French doors leading to a balcony boasted a bathroom straight out of a fantasy. A see-through fireplace, crystal chandelier, sunken marble whirlpool tub, and a his and hers vanity with brass fixtures made her feel as if she had stepped into the pages of *House Beautiful.*

Awed, she recognized that this must be the master bedroom, and turned to him. "This is gorgeous, but why did you put me here?"

He rested his hands on her shoulders. "I thought you might as well stay in the room that will be yours after we get married. Anything you don't like, you can change. Redecorate the whole damn room if you want."

She shook her head, overwhelmed at the idea of trying to improve on the perfect blend of feminine colors and fabrics and the masculinity of the dark woods and massive lines of the furniture. "Where will you be?"

"Down the hall. Here later, if you want."

How she wanted, but he was going to make it her choice. More than anything, she longed for him to wrap his strong arms around her and whisper reassurances to her that they were doing the right thing, and everything was going to be okay. Except he'd already said they couldn't share a room here at the ranch. "Your mothers–I don't think–" she let her voice trail off.

A flicker of disappointment crossed his face, but he smiled, squeezed her shoulders, then released her. "Yeah, Rosemary and Belinda would have a cow. Gretchen and Monica probably expect it; Esther, the ultimate earth mother, would want to hear about it tomorrow."

"They're certainly very different."

He snorted. "I'll say. The truly amazing thing is how well they all get along. And they like you, Ellie. You don't have to worry about it."

"I'm glad." She watched him walk to the door, taking a piece of her hopefulness with him. "Good night, Joshua."

"See you in the morning."

The door clicked softly behind him. She stood in the middle of the huge room for a few minutes, the silence pounding in her ears, then decided to take a bath in the marble tub. Half an hour later, she dragged a washcloth through apricot scented bubbles and rested her head against the back of the tub. Such luxury. She tried to imagine living here day after day, until the magnificence of her surroundings faded into ordinariness. She couldn't fathom it.

After growing up at the farm, its atmosphere a combination of austere and rustic, Belle Ranch seemed positively opulent.

Remembering the night she and Joshua had spent at the Four Seasons made her think of him sitting in the tub, feeding her ice cream, his black Stetson perched back on his head. Which made her think of …. Her face heated. The feelings he inspired were certainly not any she'd ever have dreamed she was capable of. The tub suddenly seemed too vast for one person. What a waste of water. Pulling the plug, she got out and dried off with a towel that was as big as she.

She put on a cotton gown and went to turn down the bed. A small tissue wrapped package lay on the pillow. She slowly undid the ribbon.

A pair of delicately beaded earrings nestled in the pink paper. Her breath caught in her throat. The same earrings that she'd admired at the Spring Fling. Obviously, he'd seen her pretend to try them on, but how had he known how much she'd wanted them?

He was good, she had to give him that, but then he had years of experience in knowing how to please a woman. Why did she find the thought of all the others before her so disturbing? If this was supposed to be a very straightforward arrangement, why did she feel so off balance?

Because she was falling in love with him, that's why. In other circumstances, that would be the preferred thing for the bride to do. But for her . . . . She couldn't let him have her heart, not if she wanted to survive this marriage with her dignity intact.

She stood before the cheval glass and put the earrings on, laughing at her reflection for the contrast of plain, pale blue nightgown and the dangling, iridescent earrings. Too bad Joshua couldn't see her now. I'll be here later, if you want.

She did want to be with him, more than she would have guessed, but she couldn't very well go knock on his bedroom door with his mothers and brother prowling around. What would they think? Besides, he might have gone back downstairs. She could call him on his private line, but that seemed silly when he was just a few footsteps away.

Sighing, she crawled beneath the covers and turned out the light. A cool breeze puffed the sheer window curtains in and carried soft spring scents and a faint melody.

She knew that song. "On the Verge". She remembered dancing with Joshua to that tune at the honky-tonk the night they'd met. Climbing down from the high four poster bed, she flung the French doors open and crept out onto the porch. The music was a little louder, almost as if it were piped onto the porch. Pale moonlight streamed through the post oaks. Closing her eyes, she twirled around the balcony, letting her gown billow out around her.

"You forgot your dancing shoes." Joshua's voice came out of the shadows.

Ellie stumbled, but his hand on her arm steadied her. She pressed a hand to her chest. "What are you doing?"

"Sitting here hoping you'd forget to lock your bedroom door."

She let him pull her onto his lap. "How did you get here?"

"Shimmied the drain pipe. Used to do that a lot, only down, not up."

"You could have just knocked."

"Yeah, but where's the challenge in that?" He reached up and gently touched an earring then tucked her hair behind her ear. "Pretty."

"Looking for a challenge, are you?"

He frowned. "I had enough of one trying to

escape Esther. Man, that woman's got a devious mind."

"She just knows you too well." She traced his ear with the tip of her finger. "Do you really think you should be here?"

"Hell, no." His hand slid beneath her hair, cupping the back of her neck and pulling her face a breath away from his. "We should be in there. Checking out that king size bed." His lips brushed hers, sending a shiver of anticipation through her. "If you want me to go, Ellie, I will. But all I really want to do is hold you for awhile. Promise."

"Don't make promises I might not let you keep."

"Talk about challenges, but if you insist."

His eyes were dark and impossible for her to read, but his hands clasped her waist and set her on her feet. He rose and bent to pick up a large boom box.

"Want the music inside?"

She raised her eyebrows. "Don't tell me you shimmied up the drainpipe with that thing."

"Nope. It's called planned spontaneity. I left it here this afternoon."

"Pretty sure of yourself, aren't you?" Ellie laced her fingers with his and preceded him into the bedroom.

He set the CD player on the dresser, pressed a button for continuous play, and then cupped his hands on her shoulders. "Of course. It's you I'm not sure of."

She rested her palms against his chest and gazed

up into his green eyes, expecting to see a teasing glimmer but saw only seriousness. He wasn't kidding. In fact, he looked uncertain, vulnerable. Her heart constricted.

The need to reassure him poured through her and with it a sense of relief. At last. Something she could do for him. Her fingers slowly worked the buttons on his shirt. "Can you think of anything I can do to set your mind at ease?" she teased, pressing little kisses against his chest.

"A couple dozen, but that'll do for starters." He nuzzled her hair while his hands slowly caressed her back. "You smell like heaven," he murmured against her ear.

She let her hands wander down his chest, over his flat stomach until her fingers rested over his fly. His hand pressed over hers, and she curled her fingers over the bulge throbbing beneath her touch. "You feel too wicked to be in heaven," she whispered against his mouth, then kissed him.

She pushed his shirt down his shoulders and let it fall to the floor, then undid his belt and tugged his jeans past his hips. Her fingers slid over his waist, lower, beneath the waistband of his briefs until she cupped him in her hands.

"The challenge here," he said, squeezing his eyes shut, "is not to lose it before we get a chance to get started." He drew in a sharp intake of breath as her fingers cruised the length of him. "Ellie, honey, don't you understand how you make me feel?"

"Tell me," she whispered, tilting her head back to receive his kiss.

"I'd rather show you." His hands framed her face, then his fingers slid into her hair, and he kissed her as if she were all he'd ever need. He stepped out of his jeans and briefs when she finished shoving them down his legs, and carried her to the bed, setting her down on the cool sheets before he climbed in beside her.

Gathering her close, he stroked her hair, her skin. "I really did just want to hold you."

She ran her hands down his muscled chest, over his hips and trailed her fingers along his thigh, loving the way her touch made his breath catch and his muscles tighten. "And I'm supposed to believe you?"

"Absolutely." Reaching down, he grasped the hem of her nightgown and pulled it off over her head. "And this time I'm not going to let you rush me."

"By all means," she murmured as he nipped her earlobe, then kissed the sensitive skin just below. "Take all the time you need."

His hands moved over her, caressing, stroking, and tantalizing her to move closer into his touch. She shivered with the delicious sensation of his mouth on her breasts, her shoulders as his fingers danced over her skin.

His hand smoothed over the curve of her hips, pulling her closer to his hardness. Any moment now he'd be inside her. Anticipation coiled tighter, and she held her breath, but he held her slightly away.

He stroked over her abdomen, then moved lower, caressing the inside of her thigh. His fingers slid through the nest of hair, inside the sensitive folds. She dug her nails into his shoulders and tensed.

"Joshua!"

"Shh." He pressed kisses to her temple, her forehead, then he captured her mouth. His tongue swirled around hers, coaxing, even as his fingers urged a deeper response from her. She shivered and pressed harder against his hand.

"Please–" her words emerged as a little moan in a voice she barely recognized as her own.

"I'll take care of you, Ellie." His voice was as seductive as warm blankets on a cold winter night, as reassuring as the promise of spring when the first bluebonnets appeared. One arm wrapped around her, he caressed her arm, her breast, even as his other hand continued to explore the depths of her. She trembled and clung to him, whimpering little sounds, wishing the feelings building inside would crash and take her with at the same time she wanted it to never end.

He loved the way she responded to him, the wild sweet feel of her, hovering on the precipice, ready to fall. His thumb rubbing the taut, hidden bud, his fingers plunged inside. Ellie tensed and gasped, then she surrendered, shivering and trembling in his arms. He caught her little cries inside his mouth and reveled in the way she wrapped her arms around his shoulders and hung on.

"OH!"

Her eyes were huge and luminous, her face full of surprise and wonder. He chuckled and held her closer. "My thoughts exactly."

She kissed him, a slow, deep tangle of want and need that poured through his blood until he centered himself between her legs. He plunged inside, groaning at the smooth, luscious heat of her. Until she'd told him she was pregnant, he'd almost convinced himself he'd imagined the mind-blowing feeling of being flesh to flesh with her. Almost. But this was real and a thousand times sweeter than anything he could have dreamed.

She smiled up at him, laced her fingers behind his neck and rose to meet each heated thrust, tightening around him until he felt as if he'd die from the pleasure. Her breathing quickened in time with his. Gentle hands trailed down his back, her nails lightly scraping his skin. Then she pressed against his buttocks, urging him deeper, stealing his control, giving as much as she took, and he carried her with him to paradise.

Chapter Eleven

The next morning Joshua stood in the kitchen, fixing a tray to carry up to Ellie.

Barrett entered the kitchen and observed his actions with interest. "Somebody stay up so late they didn't wake up in time to catch breakfast?"

Joshua shot him a warning look and tilted his head towards the breakfast nook where Rosemary sat enjoying a second cup of coffee.

"Is Ellie not feeling well this morning, Joshua?" Concern filled Rosemary's voice.

"She's fine, Mom. Just not a morning person. I thought I'd give her a break from having to face everybody first thing." He glared at Barrett. "You've got a big mouth, little brother," he whispered, as he picked up the tray and headed for the door.

Barrett followed. "The yellow roses are a nice touch. At least she can enjoy them if the sight of plain toast and sliced bananas makes her gag."

"Jeez, you're dense." He shook his head and started up the stairs.

"Is Ellie sick? She didn't have too much wine at dinner, did she?" Gretchen paused mid-way down the staircase and looked over the tray.

Ellie hadn't touched a drop of wine, but thankfully no one but Barrett had noticed. "No, Gretchen. We're in a hurry to get started for town. I thought it would help if I brought her something to eat."

Gretchen continued to worry, a frown puckering her forehead. "Perhaps a carrot tonic will be just the pick me up she needs. I'll whip one up for her."

"Yeah, fine. I'll come back down and get it." He rolled his eyes at Barrett as Gretchen scurried down the stairs and disappeared into the kitchen.

"If she didn't feel sick before, she will after she chugs one of those down." Barrett stood at the foot of the stairs, one hand resting on the banister.

Joshua shrugged. He'd drink it himself, if necessary. Pushing health drinks and food on everyone gave Gretchen a sense of importance he hated to take away from her. "Something on your mind?"

"She does something to you, doesn't she?"

"Gretchen? Annoys the hell out of me most of the time, but she means well." Joshua deliberately pretended to misunderstand.

Barrett chuckled. "You should see your face. For weeks you've been moping around here as if you have a burr up your butt. Then one night with Ellie here and you're acting as if you've been struck by a meteor shower. You'd think you were in love with the woman."

Joshua frowned. He definitely wasn't in love.

Hell, he didn't believe in it. How could he feel it? "Nope. I just realized that now the mommas have twice as many eligible females to throw your way. And I can sit on the sidelines and watch." He continued up the stairs, gleefully imagining Barrett's scowl follow him all the way up.

She felt like death. Ellie lay face down on the bed and squeezed her eyes shut. Usually her bouts of queasiness were the worst after lunch, although lately, they seemed to start earlier and last longer. Someone rapped on the door.

She didn't answer, afraid the slightest movement would prove disastrous.

"Ellie? It's me." Joshua's voice rang out, then the door opened. "I brought you something to eat."

"Leave it and go away," she mumbled.

Dishes rattled, then she felt his weight on the bed beside her. "You've got to eat something. That's the only thing that will help."

"Says who? Dr Seuss?" She kept her eyes closed, but didn't pull away when he took her hand.

"They were out of that one at the bookstore, so I picked up a couple of others. They all agree that expectant mothers need something on their stomachs to get over the queasiness. Come on, Ellie, sit up and eat. I want to get to Austin while the jewelers is still open."

"I've changed my mind. I don't want to marry you."

He laughed. "How could you change your mind when you didn't want to get married in the first place?"

He could laugh now, but in a few months, she was going to look like a watermelon with legs. Then he'd be the one who was sorry. She felt him move away, then he was placing a cool rag on the back of her neck.

"I forgot my crackers," she whispered.

"How about toast? Sliced bananas? A glass of milk?"

"Crackers. It's the only thing that helps."

He brushed a kiss on her hair. "Any particular kind?"

"Saltines."

"Okay, crackers it will be." He rose and moved to the door. "Anything else?"

"Gingerale."

"You've got it."

"And Joshua?"

He hesitated. "What else?"

She watched him, his broad shoulders blocking the doorway, slouching slightly so he wouldn't hit his head on the doorframe. "I really don't want to go to Austin today."

His eyes narrowed. "That's not negotiable. I'll be back in a few minutes."

The pantry yielded every conceivable kind of

cracker, except plain saltines. The wet bar held a
dozen varieties of mixers, but no gingerale. The
mothers watched, bemused, as he stalked out of the
house, car keys in hand, grumbling beneath his
breath.

Barrett insisted on going with him. "Just think.
From here it only gets better. Diapers. Two a.m.
feedings. Having to account to someone for where
you are."

Put that way, it didn't sound very appealing. Then
he was remembering last night, Ellie's soft smile,
her hands on him, the mind-melting sensation of
being wrapped in her sweet warmth. The heady
knowledge that she carried his baby.

Barrett didn't have a clue.

The Jaguar roared down the drive toward town.
"Jealous, are you?" He grinned.

Barrett groaned. "Oh, please. Have you really
stopped to think about what you're getting into?"

He had, and as balky as Ellie was, the sooner they
got married, the better. He couldn't afford to give
her time to find a way out. "She told me this
morning that she's changed her mind."

"If you spent the night in her room, that's not a
good sign."

Ignoring Barrett's gibe, he flexed his hands on the
wheel. "She's scared, Barrett. Part of it's because of
her little sister being so sick, but she'll have to face
that whether we get married or not. Something
else–"

He reached for the phone and dialed DJ's number.

After bringing his friend up to date, he made arrangements for him to priority mail the report he'd refused to give him earlier. Joshua hung up the phone.

"Why don't you ask Ellie what's bothering her?" Barrett raised a quizzical brow.

"I would if I thought she'd give me the answers I want. Damn, but she's a secretive woman."

"So have DJ fax the report, and you could talk to her about it before you bring her home tomorrow."

"Since I don't want Ellie to see it, I'd rather it arrive after she's gone."

Barrett nodded. "Makes sense. She'd probably be more likely to tell you what's bugging her if you had known her longer."

"Probably."

Silence stretched between them for several minutes, then Barrett turned slightly in his seat. "Let me give you something else to think about."

"Shoot."

"You might have to take a few steps backwards before you can go forward with this lady, regardless of the baby."

"Meaning?"

Barrett scratched his head. "It occurred to me that you two skipped a few essential steps in the getting acquainted process."

That was an understatement. They'd gone from a

casual kiss and a few dances to explosive sex to instant parenthood. "Yeah, I see what you mean. Thanks, Barrett."

Silence fell between them, but it was the comfortable quiet of two people completely at ease with one another. They were halfway back to the ranch before Barrett spoke.

"Sure you're not in love with her?"

Joshua glanced at the sack containing a box of saltines and two bottles of gingerale. He thought about the books he'd been reading ever since he found out Ellie was pregnant and the tray he'd so carefully fixed for her that she hadn't even touched. "No." He sighed. "Actually, I'm not sure I'd know how to recognize it. I just know that when I'm with her it's like I've found something I've been missing for a long time." Maybe something he'd never had before.

Which was why there was no way he was going to let her go.

A few hours later at Deeds Jewelers in the shopping mall in Austin, Joshua tried to rein in his impatience. What was so tough about picking out a ring? Ellie either couldn't or wouldn't make a decision.

She crossed her arms. "I fail to see the point in this. Maybe you don't care about spending buckets of money, but I'm just not used to living that way."

He occupied the jeweler with a discussion about carat weights and clarity and watched Ellie out of the corner of his eye. She seemed a lot more interested in the other jewelry than the wedding rings. Barrett was probably right. All that was wrong with Ellie was a case of too much too soon.

Unfortunately, they didn't have unlimited time. He wanted to be good and married before the world had to know she was pregnant.

"We can look around some more if you want. Or come back in a couple of weeks. Or I'll pick one out later and surprise you."

Her relief was a visible thing. The tiny frown lines around her eyes smoothed out as she relaxed. "Fine. Can we go to Taylor's now?"

They left the jewelry store and walked out into the mall. Saturday shoppers flowed around them.

He watched her observe the shoppers, a wistful expression on her face. "I thought you had some other errands."

"I want to get something for Lauren."

He thought for a moment. Here was his chance to surprise her. "Why don't you do that, and I'll meet you at the cookie factory in twenty minutes?"

Once she was out of sight, he returned to the jewelry store. Thinking about all the things he knew about her, the clothes she wore, the house she lived in, he narrowed down the necklaces to the one he was sure she'd liked. He would have preferred to give her a diamond ring, something that would definitively announce to the world that she was his, but that could wait a little longer. Not much, but a little.

He waited until they were in the car before he gave it to her.

"Close your eyes."

Heart pounding, Ellie complied. He wouldn't, he couldn't have returned to the jewelers to get a ring she wasn't ready to wear. Paper rustled, his breath stirred against her temple.

"Okay. Now you can look."

Dangling before her eyes was the heart shaped diamond pendant she'd secretly admired at the jewelry store. How did he manage to know what she liked when he knew so little about her?

"I'm very observant," he said, as if he'd read her mind.

"Oh, Joshua, it's beautiful." She gently touched it and watched the sun turn the diamonds into fiery light. "But you shouldn't have. I didn't even thank you for the earrings you gave me last night."

He gave her a wicked smile. "Oh, yes you did."

She felt the heat spread from her face down her neck, and he chuckled. She looked down at her lap. "You're awfully free with your money."

He placed his finger under her chin and tipped her face up to meet his gaze. "I don't spend what I don't have, if that's what you're so worried about. Can I put it on you?"

When she nodded, he undid the clasp and circled her neck with the chain. Ellie lifted her hair up so that he could fasten the delicate gold chain. "Thank you, Joshua. I really like it. It's just–I don't know what I can possibly give you in return."

He straightened the chain, letting his fingers trail down her skin to where the diamond heart nestled above her cleavage. He bent his head and kissed her, a light brush of his lips on hers. "Yes, you do."

Ellie's heart sank, but she looped her hands behind his neck and forced herself to gaze into the green depths of his eyes. "What will happen when that's not enough?"

He flashed her a wicked grin. "I find that impossible to imagine."

"I'm serious. Have you really thought about what's going to happen in a few months? Taylor told me I'd probably start showing early because I'm so small, there's no place to hide it. How are you going to like it when I look like I swallowed a watermelon?"

He smoothed his palm over her abdomen. "I can't wait. I just want to be married before then."

"Joshua–"

"Ellie, what is it going to take to convince you that I really want this baby?"

She didn't doubt that. Too bad she couldn't believe he really wanted *her*. "I won't even consider a wedding until Lauren's recovered." That would give him enough time to cool off and realize the whole idea was a bad one, especially if Lauren's operation didn't go well.

He frowned, then startled her by pulling her across his lap and proceeding to kiss her senseless until she felt as if she never wanted to leave the warmth and security of his arms. Sighing, Ellie closed her eyes, loving the way his lips caressed her neck, teased her ear, and then caught her mouth in a deep kiss that made her forget they sat in a crowded mall parking lot. Wrapping his arms around her, he held her tightly against his chest.

"Well, don't expect me not to use every devious means I can think of to persuade you otherwise."

Ellie sat in Taylor's modern kitchen, watching her fix a Caesar salad while Joshua grilled steaks on the gas grill on the redwood deck.

"Hand me the Parmesan cheese, would you?" Taylor dug into the wooden bowl, expertly coating the romaine lettuce leaves with salad dressing.

"So what do you think?"

"I like him." Taylor smiled. "He's gorgeous, Ellie. And charming."

"And bossy, and controlling. Oh, and let's not forget desperate."

"He's also generous." She gestured at Ellie's diamond necklace. "A lot of women would gladly trade places with you, and you look downright glum."

"That's because if it weren't for the baby, we wouldn't be here now."

"Maybe not as in here, at my house, but trust me. You two would still be an item. He has a way of looking at you that sends the heat index sky rocketing."

Ellie went to the refrigerator and pulled out a bowl of freshly grated cheese. "He thinks we should get married yesterday."

"So why didn't you?"

"I'm afraid he hasn't thought this whole thing through."

Taylor raised a brow. "And you have?"

Ellie sank back down on the barstool. "I know the fireworks won't last. As soon as he realizes how rough it's going to be, he'll be gone."

"Like your father?" Taylor's voice was gentle.

Ellie wrung her hands together. "Yes," she whispered.

Chapter Twelve

The patio door slid open and Joshua stuck his head inside in time to catch Ellie's stricken expression. "Steaks are about done, ladies." Whoa. Obviously a very heavy discussion was in progress. Maybe on the way home, he could pry some answers out of Ellie. Or Taylor, if the opportunity arose.

Taylor flashed him a dimpled smile. "We'll be right out. Grab the potatoes, Ellie, and I'll bring the salad."

Dinner was a light-hearted affair, and Taylor was a gracious hostess. He liked Ellie's doctor/friend a lot, but then he'd probably like anybody who held Ellie in such high esteem. He wondered if Taylor knew how he and Ellie had met. Probably not, but he had the feeling she would understand.

Afterward, they went inside and Taylor served coffee in the living room. Joshua built a fire in the rock fireplace, then sat beside Ellie on the leather sectional sofa. She curled against his side and immediately fell asleep. His hand automatically dropped down and started stroking her soft hair. He felt Taylor's steady regard before she spoke.

"So are you inside out crazy about her or are you

just trying to do the honorable thing?"

He blew out a slow breath. "Both, probably." Something more, too. Like how the dark loneliness inside him dissipated when he was with her, but he couldn't begin to explain that to Ellie's friend when he didn't understand it himself.

"She's really worried about the baby being okay. Which is understandable, considering how sick her sister has been all her life. But is it logical? I mean, what are the risks, exactly?"

Taylor shrugged. "It's hard to say. Ellie is convinced Lauren's condition is hereditary, and when it comes to genetics, she knows what she's talking about. Their mother died during what should have been a routine Caesarian, whether from actual heart failure or a reaction to the anesthetic, I don't know. The real problem is her father's medical history. And his family's. Apparently, Ellie's mother told her his family has a long history of heart disease similar to Lauren's. But since no one has seen or heard from him in ten years, that's impossible to verify, and he wasn't from around there in the first place."

"Ten years?" Joshua was appalled. How could a man walk out on his own family? "That means he left right before Lauren was born." A baby who'd arrived years after Ellie's parents thought they were finished with their family. One who was diagnosed as chronically ill just weeks after her birth. A motherless, fatherless child left to the care of her two older sisters.

Damn. No wonder Ellie didn't trust him to stick around. That explained a lot. He probably didn't need that report from DJ after all. "No one knows where her old man went?"

Taylor shook her head. "He was an over the road driver for Red Line Trucking. Just got in his rig one morning and kept on going. It was hard on all of them, but especially on Ellie. She was devastated, nearly quit college even though she only had one semester left, but Jenna insisted she finish."

Then as soon as she had, she returned to the farm to help raise Lauren where she tried to hold everything together with a wish and a prayer. Not surprising then, that she didn't want to depend on anyone else. Apparently mistaking his fierce expression, Taylor laid a hand on his arm.

"As soon as she's a little further along, we can do a lot of tests to make sure everything is progressing normally. I'm cautiously optimistic about her chances of having a healthy baby, but she needs to take extra good care of herself."

"With that in mind, we'd better be going."

"You're welcome to stay here. Ellie has a room on stand-by."

The idea was tempting, especially since here there wouldn't be any pre-dawn sneaking back to his own room, but then they'd have to go back to Belle Ranch in the morning.

"Thanks, Taylor, but I'd like to go back tonight.

Maybe next time we're in town."

"Are you two done talking about me?" Ellie mumbled, sitting up and stretching.

"Yeah, Taylor told me both stories about how wild you were in college."

"I'm surprised that didn't make you doze off." She stood and gave Taylor a hug. "Sorry for being such a lousy guest. I just feel like I could sleep around the clock."

Taylor laughed. "Goes with the territory. I'll see you at my office in a couple of weeks. Be sure to bring Joshua with you."

"I'll be her shadow," he promised. Ellie gave him a dark look, but he laughed and squeezed her shoulders.

The next morning at the ranch, Ellie sat in the parlor, surrounded by bridal magazines, fabric swatches, and five women who each thought they had the perfect plan for her and Joshua's wedding. He had wisely escaped somewhere with Barrett. Ellie wanted to scream.

"I know Joshua told you we were planning a big wedding, but I've changed my mind."

For a moment, five appalled faces turned her way. Good grief. If she told them she didn't want to marry him in the first place they'd probably chase her into the next county.

She hastened to clarify what she meant. "I prefer

to keep it very simple since that's the only way my little sister will be able to participate. Did Joshua tell you how ill she is? A family wedding where we won't have to worry about crowds of people would be best. Maybe at our farm."

Monica looked horrified.

"A wedding here would be lovely," Rosemary said, her expression dreamy. "Just think of floating down that grand staircase with Joshua waiting at the bottom to take your hand."

Ellie could picture it, too, much to her dismay. "Our farm. Just the immediate family," she insisted.

"What about the reception?" Monica pressed on. "Something elegant in Austin would be a good compromise."

Not as far as Ellie was concerned.

"We have to make sure we instruct the caterer to include some healthy choices in the buffet. Preferably a vegetarian menu." Gretchen sat forward in her chair. "Why the last wedding I attended they actually served rounds of roast beef and fried shrimp." She shuddered.

Belinda gave her a cold look. "That was my wedding, thank you very much."

Esther joined in. "We must find the perfect dress. Something that will set Joshua back on his heels. I know the perfect little dress shop–"

"Maybe Ellie would like to wear her mother's dress. That would be sweet." Belinda seemed to pick up on Ellie's distress at the thought of trying on gowns that wouldn't even fit by the time she and Joshua actually got married. If they did.

"What a marvelous idea." Rosemary clasped her hands together. "Or perhaps one of ours could be altered to fit. And Joshua's mother had a lovely gown that's boxed up somewhere in the attic."

Ellie wondered if any of them were styled after maternity gowns. She pictured herself instructing a seamstress to let out the seams to accommodate the basketball her stomach was sure to look like in another three months. "I really think–"

Joshua stuck his head in the door. "You ready to head back to the farm, Ellie? I know you said you had papers to grade before tomorrow."

She'd never been so glad to see anyone. Joshua winked at her as if guessing her thoughts. "I can be ready to go in five minutes."

"But we haven't even begun to cover the most important things. The guest list. Selecting a caterer. A florist." Monica pursed her lips. "These things take time and careful consideration if they're to be done right."

"There's always next weekend." Ellie jumped up, then bent to scoop up a few of the bridal magazines. "Thank you so much for your help. I'll take a few of these with me and look at them during the week."

"There's no time to waste here," Monica continued to bemoan the lack of lead time to plan a "proper" wedding while Ellie made her escape.

Ten minutes later, the Jaguar roared down the

driveway. Joshua's hands tightened on the wheel. "Monica was right about one thing: there's no time to waste, and we are lacking one essential ingredient."

Ellie shot him a quizzical look. He wasn't going to start harping about a ring again already, was he?

"A date, Ellie."

"I told you, not until after Lauren has her surgery."

"Which will be when?" Frustration edged his voice. "Look, we can always change it if we need to. I just want a target date. When is Lauren having her operation?"

Ellie twisted her hands in her lap. "As soon as the school year is over. If—"

"If what?"

"If we have enough money." She held up a hand. "And I swear, Joshua, if you do any more than you already have, then you can forget the whole thing. I feel like you're trying to take over my life."

He scowled. "You sure don't like to give anyone a chance to help out, do you?"

"Stop trying to buy me!"

He scratched his head and pretended to act puzzled. "Now what on earth would have given me the idea you were for sale?"

Ellie covered her face with her hands in a futile attempt to hide the hot color racing over her skin. "That's a rotten thing to say."

He sighed deeply, reached over and took her

hand. "You're right. I didn't mean it, and you know it. You just frustrate the hell out of me."

It was all too tempting to give in to the desire to take his comfort and support. Ellie stared at the rolling hills zipping past the window. If she wasn't careful, she would be so hopelessly wrapped up in his life and he in hers, she wouldn't be able to breathe.

"Why didn't you ask Taylor to help you out instead of going to that honky-tonk? Not that I'm sorry you did."

"I can't take any more from her. She's done so much for me already, and she's got her own problems. Medical school loans, start-up costs for her practice, her new house. It's bad enough to be her indigent patient. I can't ask her to help subsidize Lauren's medical care as well."

"How much more do you need?"

"Twenty thousand dollars." It might as well be a million. She didn't have a clue as to how they could raise more than Mandy's fund raising efforts had already gathered. Certainly even Joshua didn't have that kind of cash lying around with the terms of his father's will restricting his access to any of the family assets. Even if he did, she wouldn't take another dime from him.

Joshua tapped his fingers on the steering wheel and was silent for several minutes. "We'll figure something out. Make the appointments for Lauren, then give me a date for when you think you'll be home from Cleveland. We can have the wedding at the farm if that's what will make you happy."

Ellie blinked back tears. What would make her happy was to think he was doing this for her. Because he loved her, not just because she was a means to an end for him.

Two weeks later, Joshua sat in his office going over the production reports. His intercom beeped.

"You have a visitor." Mrs Higgins voice was crisply efficient. "Do you have time to see Daniel Hirsch, or shall I have him make an appointment?"

Ellie's neighbor. What was he doing here? "No, I'll see him. Send him in."

Danny stood in the door, looking as nervous as a barnyard rat confronting the cat. "Hey, Joshua. Hope I'm not interrupting."

Joshua rose and motioned him towards a conversational grouping of leather overstuffed chairs. "No problem. Coffee?"

Danny nodded. Looking less than pleased, Mrs Higgins pursed her lips, but left.

They chatted a few minutes about the weather, the crop Danny was wanting to put in once the rain let up. Mrs Higgins returned with a tray containing a silver carafe of coffee, sugar, creamer, and mugs bearing the Mama Belle logo.

After she closed the door, Joshua turned to Danny. "Okay, so what's up? I know you didn't

drive all the way over here to discuss the weather. Ellie and the girls all right?"

"Yeah, fine." Danny gulped a scalding mouthful of coffee. "Didn't mean to worry you. It's just–what I've got to tell you has to be strictly confidential. No way do I want the girls knowing about this."

"Sure." His curiosity thoroughly aroused, Joshua forced himself to lean back in his chair and sip his coffee. "Something I can help you with?"

"You bet." Danny set down his mug, then dug into his pocket, withdrawing a huge wad of bills. "I think this will fill the gap in what they're needing for Lauren's surgery."

Reluctantly, Joshua let him hand over the money. He leafed through it. "There must be–"

"Yes, sir. Twenty thousand dollars." Danny's voice held a note of pride. "Had to do some finagling, sell off a few things, but I figured it was way past time I chipped in to help my little girl."

His little girl. Joshua couldn't help but smile. Despite the fact that Lauren was a trifle precocious, she was a darling child everyone couldn't help but love. Ellie was doing a terrific job raising her. She was going to be a fantastic mother. Too bad she was dead set against the idea of having more than one. Maybe . . .

Danny's expression was a mixture of relief and defiance, giving Joshua the certainty he'd somehow missed the point. He must want reassurance that Joshua wouldn't tell the girls where the rest of the money had come from. Which wouldn't be easy since Ellie didn't want it coming from him either.

Danny gripped the arms of the chair and looked as if he were ready to either bolt from the room or spill his guts.

Joshua rubbed his chin. "There something else you wanted to tell me?"

"It doesn't take a brain surgeon to figure out the only reason Ellie Winfield would get married when she's been so dead set against it is because she's pregnant. Then Jenna is mighty worried about her–partly because of their momma, partly because Lauren's heart condition is inherited. I think you deserve to know you don't need to worry."

"Are you going to tell me why?"

Danny's knuckles turned white from his tense grip. "I promised Louise I'd never tell the girls, so this has got to stay in this room."

"If that's what you want." Joshua tensed, waiting for Danny to continue.

Danny's expression was that of a man being tortured by slow degrees. "You've no idea how hard it's been, watching them struggle, seeing my baby suffer and not being able to take my place as her daddy."

"Hold it." His little girl. Wait a minute. Was Danny telling him . . . . Joshua had the feeling he'd walked into the middle of a movie drama. "Are you saying what I think you are?"

"You can't blame their momma. Louise was

lonely, what with her husband gone more than he was there, both of her girls off to college. She was a beautiful woman. Things just–happened."

Joshua looked at Danny as if for the first time and tried to imagine him eleven years ago. Joshua's age now. He'd seen pictures of Louise Winfield. Ellie's mother was about ten years older than Danny and had looked like Ellie would in another thirteen or so years. Stunning. Classy and full of fire. "Holy shit. You're Lauren's father?"

"We never imagined there'd be such a price to pay." Danny plucked at an imaginary piece of lint on his faded jeans. "Ellie's daddy never knew the baby was mine. He just knew it wasn't his and couldn't live with that. So he took off. Louise never got over it."

Danny continued, his words flowing like a river breaking through a dam. "I can't have my own family, living on borrowed time as it were. Kind of had one foot in the grave and the other on a banana peel ever since I was about Ellie's age."

Joshua sat back in his chair and simply stared. Lauren was Ellie's half sister. Her health problems were from a father they didn't share. Here was the reassurance Ellie needed so desperately, and he'd never be able to tell her. Blast it, anyway.

"Being with Louise was like a reprieve sent from heaven," Danny said softly.

Joshua knew that feeling all too well. "Don't you think it's time Ellie and Jenna, hell, Lauren especially know this?"

Danny shook his head, a determined glint in his suspiciously moist eyes. "Ellie and Jenna think the world of their mother. I can't let her memory be tarnished to them. And if you try—" he spread his hands in a challenging gesture, "who do you think they're going to believe?"

Not him, Joshua realized with a sinking heart. Why was it that when the best solution presented itself, one often found there was no way to use it?

Chapter Thirteen

"Take the money, Ellie." Joshua handed her a check made out to the trust fund established for Lauren.

"Joshua Bellinghausen, I thought I told you I couldn't accept any more money from you." Mad enough to spit barbed wire, Ellie rested her hands on her hips.

Joshua pressed the check into her hand. "It's not from me, I swear, although I was about to sell the Jaguar just so we could get this over with."

He made it sound like he was scheduling a dental appointment, not planning a wedding.

"Thanks a lot, Romeo."

"Anybody tell you what a grouch you're getting to be?" He wrapped his arms around her and bent his head to nibble on her earlobe.

"You. Constantly." Ellie suppressed a shiver and let herself relax into his arms. When he held her like this, she could almost convince herself that he really did care for her, that everything would be as it should for two people committing their lives to each other. Almost. "Were you really thinking about selling the Jaguar?"

"Yes, ma'am." His lips left her ear to travel down

her neck. Ellie's knees turned to putty. "I can't picture a car seat in the back. Somehow ruins the image."

The carefree bachelor. Ellie tensed. "We wouldn't want that, now would we?"

"Certainly not." He rubbed her back, coaxing her further into his embrace. "I meant the car's image. You've already ruined mine."

"Is that right?" She snuggled into him, willing to take whatever moments fate allowed. It surprised her how much she missed seeing him during the week, although he called her every night before she went to sleep. She wasn't sure why he did. They never had much to say and sometimes the silence stretched awkwardly between them. Maybe it was a sign of what was to come if they actually did get married. Joshua's insistence they wed hadn't lessened in the intervening weeks.

"The car was my dad's pride and joy, Ellie. Not mine. I'm more than ready to go back to my Bronco. I'm tired of driving a car that squashes my hat."

"That's okay. Your big head will keep it from flattening out."

He chuckled. "It really sets my mind at ease to know I've so thoroughly charmed you. When's the last day of school?"

"Next Wednesday. We leave for Cleveland the day after that."

"I'm going with you."

Ellie placed her palms against his chest and looked up at him. "No, you're not. I'll have my hands full with Lauren and Jenna. I don't need you there distracting me."

He cradled her face in his hands. "I wasn't planning on distracting, I want to be there for you."

Her heart squeezed. How she wanted to believe him. She was so tired of lugging all the emotional burdens around by herself, but if he really understood just what she was up against, he'd leave. Like her father had when her mother had needed him so badly.

"The little guy's going to be okay, Ellie. And so will you."

"Have it on the highest authority, do you?"

His eyes had a peculiarly guarded look. "Something like that."

"Why are you so certain it's going to be a boy?"

He grinned. "The Bellinghausens haven't had a girl baby for three generations."

"Well, the Ellisons haven't had a boy for four," she retorted. "So put that in your Stetson."

He released her and wandered to the window. "Is Danny going to watch the farm?"

She went to stand beside him. Outside, Jenna pulled weeds from the flower beds. Lauren alternately helped and sat on the porch drinking a glass of lemonade while Danny mowed the patch of grass surrounding the house. "I feel like we impose endlessly on him, but he says he doesn't mind helping out." She sighed. "Still–"

"He wouldn't do it if he didn't want to." His voice held a rough edge of impatience. Ellie looked up at him in surprise. He was so steadfastly calm, no matter how she needled him. Had she pushed him too much?

He draped his arm over her shoulders and fingered the gold chain that held her diamond necklace, barely caressing her skin from her neck down to where the heart nestled just above her cleavage. "Your worst problem is your absolute refusal to let anybody else do the giving. What are we going to do to cure you of that?"

Her gaze locked with the smoky heat of his, but before she could respond, he'd scooped her up into his arms as if she weighed no more than a feather and headed for the stairs.

Ellie looped her arms around his neck as he took the stairs two at a time. Her heart pounded wildly. He wouldn't. Not with her family just outside. "Joshua, what are you doing?"

"Taking care of Ellie."

"But Jenna. Lauren."

He grinned. "I think even a ten year old can figure out what a locked bedroom door means."

She searched for an excuse he might buy. "I thought we were going to spend the weekend at the ranch."

He shrugged. "We may. We may not. We'll see what we want to do tomorrow. But tonight–" he waggled his brows at her.

"Joshua!"

He shoved her bedroom door open with his
shoulder. The shades drawn, a fat candle flickered,
sending out an aroma of cinnamon and spice. Ellie
twisted to see what he'd managed to set up. The
comforter on the bed had been pulled back and a
thick towel spread over the cotton sheets. A push of
his foot shut the door, then he slid the bolt home.
Gently, he set her on her feet.

"Now, lady, are you going to disrobe quietly, or
do I have to strip you myself?"

"I think you should do it," she said, forcing away
her misgivings and letting herself be caught up in
his playful mood.

His fingers nimbly worked the buttons running
down the front of her flowered dress. "I promise I
don't have anything perverse in mind."

"Too bad," she teased, standing on tiptoe to nip
his lower lip.

"Not yet, anyway." He slowly removed the rest of
her clothes. When she was naked, he carefully undid
her necklace and set it on the dresser, then again
picked her up and placed her on the bed. "Roll
over."

"What?!"

He chuckled as he removed his watch and the
heavy signet ring he wore, then poured something
into the palm of his hand. "Close your eyes and be
still, like the good little girl I know you're not."

"Very funny." She rolled onto her stomach and closed her eyes, then his hands were on her neck, her shoulders, working magic and scented oil into the tense muscles. Soothing, caressing, his fingers kneaded down the length of her spine, massaged her lower back, her buttocks. "I don't even want to think about where you learned how to do this."

"Hush." He brushed a kiss against the side of her face. "Talking to your masseur is a sure way to disrupt his concentration. Next thing you know, he'll be aroused. And that's not on the program at the moment."

"You're sure about that," she murmured drowsily. The thought of his hard flesh against hers, slick with heat and arousal was delicious. She let the images pour through her mind and ignite a slow fire in the pit of her stomach.

His hands moved down her legs. She'd never felt anything like this before: a combination of eroticism and relaxation that was intoxicating. Drugging. She almost felt as if she were floating on a heated cloud of desire and pleasure.

His thumb pressed into her instep, then the soles of her feet. The touch of his hands on her calves, and then her thighs made her catch her lower lip between her teeth to stifle a longing sigh. The drone of the lawn mower drifted in through the window. Lauren's childish laugh seemed to come from a long way off.

She barely had the energy to roll onto her back. A

soft cloth covered her eyes. His hands continued massaging her arms, feathered around her breasts, the tease of his touch almost agonizing. He smoothed his palm over the barely perceptible swell of her abdomen. "Why, Miss Winfield. I do believe you're starting to show."

"Hmm. Too much of Rosemary's strudel, that's all."

"I don't think so." She could hear the smile in his voice.

"From here it only gets worse."

"I disagree. Better."

She wanted to see his expression but couldn't muster the energy to remove the cloth covering her eyes. Surely, he was joking. How could a man who enjoyed women as much as Joshua apparently did think there was anything sexy about being pregnant? "You won't say that in another six months." If he was even still around then.

"Having a man's baby is the ultimate in sexy, sugar." Unexpectedly, his mouth covered hers. Drowning in sensations, the texture of his tongue on hers, the rasp of whiskers on her chin, the scent of oil and his cologne, the pressure of his hands on her shoulders, Ellie slid her arms around him and felt his heart pound in tandem with her own. Her breath caught in her throat.

"Your shirt is going to be ruined, if you don't take it off," she whispered when he dragged his mouth from hers.

He clasped her hands and kissed the tips of her fingers before backing away. "Don't think you don't tempt me, but this isn't about what I want: it's about what you need." He drew the sheet over her and turned away. "I'll be back."

A short time later, Ellie soaked in the bath he'd drawn for her and sipped a mug of orange-spice tea laced with honey. Sounds and aromas of dinner preparations wafted up from downstairs. Joshua's deep voice mingled with Lauren's childish laugher and Jenna's softer tones. She wished she could hear what they were talking about. As much as she relished luxuriating in a bubble bath, she was lonely. Not just for conversation, for Joshua.

How ridiculous. She managed just fine all week long without him, why should she miss him when he was merely downstairs?

Why hadn't he made love to her? As much as she'd enjoyed the massage, the warm feelings of arousal still burned deep inside. She had stressed to him the importance of maintaining proper appearances for Lauren's sake, but her own inhibitions vanished about the time his hands started kneading her buttocks. Besides, Lauren and Jenna had still been outside when she'd navigated on shaky legs from her bedroom to the bathroom and climbed into the tub.

Certainly her sisters, especially Jenna, would have the sense to respect a locked door. Maybe later . . . .

She dragged a washcloth through the apricot scented bubbles. Maybe he wasn't planning on staying the night. He might have decided on returning to Belle Ranch alone.

Her spirits evaporated with the bubbles. She pulled the plug on the tepid water and stepped out of the claw-footed tub. A short rap on the door stirred her anticipation. She wrapped herself in a towel, but she flung the door open to find Lauren holding a small plate of bugs on a log: celery sticks stuffed with cottage cheese and topped with raisins.

"Joshua said you were hungry, Ellie." Lauren handed her the plate. "I made these myself."

"Thank you, sweetie. They look delicious." Ellie tucked in the top edge of her towel and set the plate on the counter. "What is he doing right now, Buttercup?" She bit into a celery stick and steeled herself to be told he had already left or was in the process of heading out the door.

"Cooking dinner." Lauren cleared a spot on the mirror and inspected her mouth. "How come my tooth is taking so long to grow in?"

Cooking? "Probably because you need to drink more milk." Ellie finished drying off and stepped into a jumpsuit made of a soft, plushy fabric.

Lauren made a face. "I don't like milk. I'd rather have triple chocolate ice cream."

Ellie ruffled her hair. "I'm sure you would. However, you have to eat an awful lot of ice cream to get enough calcium to grow good bones and teeth."

"Joshua said if I come to live at Belle Ranch I can have ice cream for breakfast."

"Oh, he did." A flutter of annoyance that he'd felt he could determine her sister's actions was tempered by the pleasant picture of Lauren moving to the ranch with her. Why would Joshua tell Lauren she could come live at the ranch without discussing it with her first? Was he really willing to open his home to her entire family? What about Ellison Farms?

"Um, hmm." Lauren finished inspecting her teeth, made a face at herself, then gave Ellie a quick hug before she skipped out the door. "Joshua said to tell you that dinner is ready."

"What did he fix?" She pictured a simple supper of canned soup and toasted cheese sandwiches.

Lauren shrugged. "Some funny kind of noodle stuff." She wrinkled her nose. "It has vegetables in it."

Mother's lace tablecloth, good china, and crystal arrayed the dining room table. Ellie hesitated in the doorway. Jenna, her face glowing, looked up from laying a knife beside a plate. Mother's sterling silver. A large cut glass bowl of spinach salad sat on the sideboard along with small loaves of brown bread and a plate of fruit.

"What are you doing, Jenna?"

"We haven't eaten in the dining room in years. Joshua thought it would be fun for Lauren."

"Oh, really? Isn't that overkill for a simple supper?"

Joshua emerged from the kitchen, a huge bowl of pasta primavera in his hands. "You're just in time."

It looked to her like she was a little too late. Did he have to take over everything? She was the one who was supposed to be in charge.

Joshua set the bowl down and held a chair out for Ellie. Reluctantly, she took a seat. She'd never felt so useless in her life.

"I thought you ladies could use a break. Especially you, sugar," he whispered close to her ear.

Ellie's heart made a funny little leap. Immediately, she felt ashamed for her momentary pangs of resentment and grudging acceptance of Joshua's help. How very sweet he was. No one had fussed over her in years. Not since….

Tears stung her eyes as she remembered how her father had made such a production of hers and Jenna's birthdays. He may have been on the road most of the time, but when he'd been home, he'd known how to keep his girls happy, which made it all the more difficult to accept his abandonment, even after ten years.

She reached for her water goblet and took a hasty gulp. Glancing up, she caught Joshua's speculative gaze on her, but he squeezed her shoulder, then took his own place at the table without saying anything else.

Dinner was a light-hearted affair, with Joshua entertaining all of them with stories about the people who made Bellinghausens ice cream, and his and Barrett's growing up with six mothers taking turns trying to run their lives. Lauren, normally a very picky eater, gobbled everything in sight.

"Slow down, Buttercup. You don't want to get a tummy ache." Ellie rested her hand on her little sister's arm.

"You're such a mother hen, Ellie." Jenna surprised Ellie by speaking up. "She's fine. It's good to see her with an appetite for a change."

"Joshua is a better cooker than you are," Lauren spoke around a mouthful of noodles and vegetables.

Stung, Ellie sat back in her chair. Just because she didn't have time to cook a gourmet meal didn't mean Joshua would be able to do it on a daily basis either.

He laughed. "I'm afraid you've seen the extent of my talents, Lauren. Rosemary insisted Barrett and I learn to cook one good meal. The only other cooking I do is grilling a steak, and that's only if you like it medium rare."

Lauren wrinkled her nose. "I don't like steak. You have to chew it a hundred times before you can swallow."

Chuckling, he rose and began clearing the table,

insisting Jenna and Ellie remain. "Any one want coffee with dessert?"

Ellie wiped her mouth on a linen napkin and carefully folded the cloth before placing it beside her plate. The effects of the massage, the hot bath and too much food combined to make her so woozy with drowsiness she wished she could just rest her head on the table. "Nothing for me, thanks Joshua. I'm going to go to bed." She held her hand out to Lauren. "And I think you need to do the same, young lady."

Lauren immediately began to pout. "It's Friday night, and it's not even dark out. I'm tired of being treated like a baby. And Joshua brought my favorite flavor of ice cream."

Too weary to argue, Ellie bent and kissed the top of her head. "Then he can sit up with you when you get that tummy ache I warned you about. Good night, everyone." She stuck her head in the kitchen where Joshua stood at the sink rinsing off plates. How could he look like such a tempting hunk of masculinity while immersed in so much domesticity? "Thanks for dinner. It was terrific."

"Want me to tuck you in later?" His eyes, dark with meaning, met hers.

All too aware of Jenna and Lauren sitting behind her, she placed a finger to her lips and shook her head. "Will I see you in the morning?"

He gave her a puzzled look. "Yeah. Why wouldn't you?"

"Oh. I just didn't know if you planned on going back to the ranch tonight."

"I plan on sacking out on the daybed in the parlor unless—"

"That's fine," she interrupted. "Good night."

Two hours later, practically hoarse from alternately reading aloud and entertaining Lauren with stories about him and Barrett growing up on Belle Ranch, Joshua turned out the light in Lauren's room. He was exhausted, but at least she was finally asleep. If Ellie had to deal with this every day, it was no wonder she didn't think she had room in her life for anyone else. At least at the ranch she wouldn't have to worry about meals as they had a cook who handled all the kitchen responsibilities.

The baby was going to take all her attention, though, unless she agreed to hire a nanny. Somehow that didn't fit with what he knew about Ellie. He hoped she would have a little energy left over for him once in a while. As soon as they had a date down for the wedding, he wanted her to start thinking about which room she wanted to convert to a nursery. He imagined the smaller room across from the master bedroom done up in blues. Maybe some cowboy or train wallpaper would be cute.

One thing at a time. First he had to get her down the aisle. Quietly, he turned the knob of her bedroom door. As his eyes adjusted to the darkness, he made out her still form on the double bed. The room was silent except for the slow, even rhythm of her breathing. "Ellie?" he whispered.

No answer. Anticipation crashed. He had hoped that here he could find a way to spend the night holding her, but that was probably pretty unrealistic considering her sister. Weeknights sleeping alone were easier to deal with when he knew he had the weekends to look forward to. Remembering how tired she'd looked at dinner, he didn't have the heart to wake her. Certainly, he could keep the emptiness at bay one more night. He eased the door closed and headed down the stairs to the parlor and the narrow, lonely bed.

The vivid sensation of Joshua's hands on her skin woke her. A sense of loss sweeping over her when she realized she was alone, Ellie shifted onto her back and stared at the ceiling. A dream. So real her skin tingled with anticipation. She glanced at the clock. Midnight. She'd been asleep for hours. Where was Joshua?

She threw back the covers, rose and tugged her jumpsuit on. After opening the door, she listened carefully, but heard only the sound of a household at rest; the tick of the hall clock, the creak of wind sifting through the trees outside the window. Jenna wasn't much for staying up and had probably gone to bed around ten as she always did. Hopefully she hadn't let Lauren stay up that late. She needed to be well rested when they went to Cleveland in a week.

Ellie tiptoed down the stairs. A light burned in the study. Joshua must still be awake. Pushing open the door, she found he'd opened the daybed to its king-size width and stretched out crosswise on it, completely occupying it from corner to corner. Shirtless, one arm shading his eyes, he lay on his back, the open book on his chest rising and falling with his even breathing. Pregnancy and Childbirth. So he'd raided her bookshelves. Ellie picked up the book, startled to realize it wasn't one of hers.

She set it in his open overnight case on top of another paperback titled Massage for Couples. For the first time, she wondered if maybe Joshua's reputation as a love-and-leave-em bachelor was overstated, his previous reluctance to get involved a self-protective measure, not a selfish one.

After closing and locking the door, she sank down on the edge of the daybed. For a man who claimed he didn't know what love was, he sure was working hard to find ways to please her. Why would he do that if he didn't have some feelings for her?

He looked peacefully asleep, and she hated to disturb him after he'd worked so hard all evening so that she could relax for a change. She picked up the blanket from the foot of the bed and covered him. Leaning down, she brushed a kiss against the corner of his mouth.

His fingers circled her wrist and pulled her down

hard against his chest. Her breath rushed out in a startled little cry.

Sleepy green eyes regarded her. "Took you long enough."

"How would you know? You've been dead to the world."

"As you should be. What are you doing wandering around in the middle of the night instead of getting your rest?"

"It's pretty tough to sleep when your body is on fire." Sprawled across him, she feathered little kisses on his face.

"Tell me about it. I've been having that problem for about two months now." His hands stroked over the soft fabric of her lounging pajama-style jumpsuit. "What the hell is this thing you're wearing?"

"It's comfortable." She pressed a kiss to his mouth. "Especially with no underwear beneath it."

Heat flared in his eyes. "I knew I liked it. And it's got this very convenient zipper instead of all those teeny tiny buttons you seem to like." He eased the zipper down just far enough to slide his hands inside, skimming over her breasts in a deliciously tormenting caress. She closed her eyes and let her head drop.

"You know, I've had about enough of this."

"What?" Her eyes flew open.

He tugged the jumpsuit off one shoulder and raised his head to nibble on her shoulder. "This weekends only visitation and then sneaking around in the dead of night. I want to fall asleep holding you and wake up with you in my arms."

The thought was wildly appealing at the same time it filled her with panic. What if she got used to having him beside her only to wake up one morning to find him gone?

"Now that you've got Lauren's surgery scheduled, there's no reason not to set a wedding date."

"She's going to need time to recuperate."

"She can do that at Belle Ranch. My mothers would love it."

Straddling his hips, she planted her hands on his bare chest and regarded him. "I keep thinking you're going to change your mind."

He narrowed his eyes. "Thinking? Or hoping?"

For a moment, she thought she saw a flash of insecurity totally at odds with his reputation and his seemingly boundless self-confidence. Her nurturing instincts kicked into high gear despite her best efforts to remain unaffected.

What could she say to reassure him that wouldn't leave her own heart exposed and vulnerable? "You're expecting me to make a lot of changes. I'll have to leave the farm I grew up on—one that's been in my family for over a hundred years. You said Lauren can come with me, but is that fair to her?"

"It's obvious Lauren's life revolves around you. Why would it matter where she lives? And you told me the farm technically belongs to Jenna. How do you know she's not going to decide she wants to have her own family someday soon?"

The idea was even more preposterous than her own impending marriage. "I–" she didn't even know what to say.

"You must believe that the surgery is going to be a turning point for Lauren or you wouldn't be risking everything you hold dear to see it happen. She's going to grow up, Ellie. What are you and Jenna going to do if you have no other life?"

He sighed and rezipped her jumpsuit, placed his hands on her waist and shifted her around so she lay on her back snuggled against him. He nuzzled her neck, then reached up and shut off the light.

Darkness enfolded them, cozy and reassuring, inviting confidences. "I promised Mama I would always look after Lauren. And the farm. Family tradition says it goes to the eldest daughter, but Jenna's not interested in doing what it takes to keep it going. They need me."

"So do we, darlin'." His hand settled over the slight swelling of her abdomen, reminding her of his permanent right to share in her life and the obligation she had to give her child the family he or she deserved.

For the second time that day, Ellie wondered why he didn't make love to her. He lay on his side, pressed close to her, and she knew he wanted to.

The rigid heat of his erection burned through her clothes.

Once again, he seemed to read her mind. "Yeah, I want you, darlin'. But if it kills me, I'm going to prove to you that there's more going on here than two people with terrific fireworks between them."

She longed to tell him she loved him, but held back, unwilling to give him that kind of power over her. Bad enough that she loved him with all her heart. If he knew she did, he'd never let up on the pressure to bend her to his will. "I want what's best for our child, but I can't turn my back on what I promised Mama. If I weren't pregnant–" she trailed off.

"I'd still want to be with you." His hand caressed her abdomen, then glided higher to tantalize her breasts. A slow fire ignited deep inside her.

"Why?"

His sigh held a mixture of frustration and puzzlement. "I don't know. I just know that whatever's been gnawing at me since my father died goes away when I'm with you. Especially when we make love. That's why I took the chance I did that first night. I needed that connection with you one more time."

"I thought I was dreaming."

He chuckled. "Me, too. Felt too good to be a dream, though."

She turned in his arms and looped her arms around his neck, pulling his face close for a long

kiss. "Show me again, so this time I'll know for
certain it wasn't a dream."

"Ellie–"

She nibbled on his lower lip. "This doesn't have
to be about what you think I need–it can be about
what I want."

His hands smoothed over her back, cupped her
buttocks and pressed her tightly against him. "I want
that, too. It's just–I don't want you to think that's all
there is between us." His tongue tickled her ear. "I
like doing things for you. You seem to find it so
unexpected."

Only because she was unaccustomed to being on
the receiving end. "I've been little Miss Helper
since the day I was born."

"So assist me in getting you out of this interesting
outfit you've got on." He helped her wiggle out of
the jumpsuit, then pulled off his sweatpants and
briefs. When they were both naked, he turned her so
she lay spoon fashion against him. "It started out
like this," his warm breath tickled her ear, sending a
shiver through her. "I think we both dozed off, but
I'm guessing you fell into an exhausted slumber."

"Um, hmm." She wriggled against the hard heat
of him.

He drew in a sharp intake of breath. "Careful.
That's what you did the last time and look what it
got us."

"Are you sorry?" Her words emerged as a little
gasp as his fingers found the sensitive area between

her thighs and began the magical caressing that soon had her body, still warm and pliant from the massage, humming.

"No way." His lips moved over the back of her neck, nipping little kisses that made her rock against him. Hot and aching, she arched her back to press more firmly against his erection. She remembered feeling this way, trembling with longing, yearning so intensely she nearly wept. How could she have convinced herself it wasn't real? Then he was easing inside, filling her.

Her world began to crumble with the first sweet stroke. He wrapped his arm around her waist and pushed deep within her, murmuring little endearments as he glided in, withdrew partway and buried himself over and over. Ellie tensed and cried out, falling over the edge into a haze of warmth and languor and taking him with her.

Chapter Fourteen

Ellie snuggled close against him, drifting, loving the cozy feeling of being in his arms, the rightness of holding him deep within her. If this was what it would be like to be with him every night, then that's what she wanted with all her heart.

She heard rapping and her name called from a long way off and struggled to push away the fuzzy layers of sleep.

"Ellie? Ellie!" Jenna's frantic voice called through the locked door.

Joshua muttered and tightened his arms around her. Mortified to realize her sister stood on the other side of the door while she lay naked with him still pressed deeply inside her, Ellie wriggled away and evaded his sleepy attempt to recapture her.

What had she been thinking of? She should be in her own room, where her sisters could find her immediately if they needed her.

Something must be terribly wrong or Jenna would be too embarrassed to disturb them.

Lauren.

"I'll be right there, Jenna." She slid off the bed, groping through the bedclothes for her jumpsuit.

"Funny, you ran off last time, too," Joshua

mumbled, turning on the light and running a hand through his hair. "That doesn't say much for my technique. Looking for this?" He pulled her clothes from under the covers.

Ellie snatched her outfit from his hands and struggled to find the leg openings, hopping on one foot and poking the other into one leg of the jumpsuit. "Lauren must be sick."

Suddenly alert, Joshua stood and began fumbling for his own clothes. Ellie's pale, stricken face told him more than he wanted to know about just how serious the situation was. "Does this happen often?"

She shook her head, her blonde hair tumbling wildly around her shoulders. "I've been so afraid. She needs that surgery desperately. We've been taking a huge risk by waiting. If her heart gives out– I shouldn't have–"

"Shh. It'll be okay." He helped her find the armholes, then zipped up the suit. "Scoot. I'll be there in a couple of minutes."

He found her in the upstairs hall, gathering Lauren into her arms, ready to scoop her up. He put a hand on her arm. "Hold on a minute, sugar. Let me carry her."

"I've done this plenty." Ignoring him, she bent over the child. Lauren clutched her tummy.

"Ellie," his voice has harsh with the effort it took to control his temper. "There is no way you should be lugging a sixty pound child around."

Eyes narrowed, Ellie gave him a jerky nod and let

him pick Lauren up.

"Do we need to get her to the hospital?"

Jenna burst into the hallway. "Dr Holton said to meet him at his office, and he'll get in touch with the cardiologist. Then if he thinks it's necessary we'll have to get her to the hospital as fast as we can."

Joshua laid his hand on Ellie's shoulder. "We'll take the Jag. It'll be faster."

"Jenna and I will take Lauren in the pick-up."

Why was she so hell-bent on leaving him out of this? "Jenna can follow in the pickup. Let's go." He took Lauren and hurried out to the car. Ellie was right on his heels.

"Joshua, there is no reason for you to come with us."

"I disagree." Settling Lauren across Ellie's lap, he stalked around to the driver's side, got in and started the engine. As they headed down the driveway, the headlights of the old pickup bounced off the rearview mirror.

He glanced over at the child clutching Ellie and whimpering. Ellie's face was drawn and pale. "What happened?"

"Jenna found her on the floor outside my room." She stared out the side window, her voice flat. "She needed me and I wasn't there."

Ah, hell. A setback they couldn't afford. Not only did Ellie have to worry about her sister, she obviously felt like it was her fault just because she had chosen to come to him instead of remaining in her own room. So much for his noble intentions. He'd be better off if he'd just parked himself in that double bed with her.

He reached over to take her hand. "It's not your fault. Now quit feeling guilty, and let's just concentrate on getting her help."

Twenty minutes later, Joshua sat in the waiting room of the family doctor's office in Blanco. Jenna, her expression tight, sat across from him, her hands folded in her lap. Ellie had gone into the examining room with Lauren.

"Are you sure you want to live like this?"

Live like what? Constantly on the alert for a sick child, or damned to hover on the periphery of Ellie's pain? He was just a little bit tired of being told he couldn't handle either. "Well, now, Jenna," he drawled. "Suppose you tell me what my other options are."

Before she could speak, the door opened and Ellie emerged, looking drained, but considerably more relaxed. He stood, wanting nothing more than to take her in his arms and reassure her. Ignoring him, she sank into the chair beside Jenna and embraced her sister.

"She's okay, Jen. Just a bad case of indigestion. Poor little thing, she's as frightened as we are." She glanced up at Joshua. "We'll be leaving for Cleveland on the first available flight. Dr Holton is going to call the doctor there first thing in the

morning and get her surgery moved up. The anxiety
is draining all of us."

"I'm going with you, Ellie."

She stood and glared up at him, but he figured it
was just from the strain of the past hour. "No,
you're not. Now let's take Lauren home."

The first streaks of dawn painted the sky pink by
the time Ellie got Lauren settled into bed. For a long
time she sat on the edge of the bed, holding her
hand, waiting for her to fall asleep. She ached with
fatigue but there was so much needing to be done.
Arranging to leave school before the term was up,
packing, talking to Danny about tending the farm
while they were gone.

Breaking up with Joshua.

She smoothed back a lock of Lauren's hair. He
had nearly convinced her that they could make
things work, but after last night, she knew she
couldn't go through with it. The look of concern and
fear in his eyes had broken her heart. Had he been
wondering if they would face similar crises with
their own child? Did he now realize why she could
never risk having another one?

She loved him too much to condemn him to a life
of worrying and waiting.

Tears stung her eyes, but the longer she watched
Lauren sleep the stronger her resolve became.
Joshua deserved better, no matter how much he

acted like marrying her and being part of her family had been what he wanted all along. She intended to see that he got the chance to find someone more suitable, someone he could have a healthy family with.

Chapter Fifteen

Ellie left Lauren resting and found Joshua in the kitchen, brewing a pot of coffee and trying to interest Jenna in eating the bacon and eggs he was cooking. "I thought you said you could only cook two things." She pulled out a chair at the kitchen table and accepted the mug of coffee he handed her.

"Breakfast doesn't count. That's simply a survival skill." He smiled and set a plate with toast on the table. "You look beat."

Jenna pushed her chair back. "I'm going back to bed. Wake me if you need me."

When she'd left, Ellie quietly sipped her coffee, waiting for the right moment to tell Joshua of her decision. He stood at the stove, radiating confidence and self-assurance. How she enjoyed watching him, as at home at the farm as he was at Belle Ranch. He was the kind of man who could settle in anywhere and look at ease. He tugged at her heart, made her hands tremble.

How she loved him.

He placed a plate of eggs and bacon in front of her and took the seat next to hers.

Ellie smiled and tried to find enough interest to eat, but her stomach leaped around under the weight of what she needed to say.

He slathered peanut butter on a piece of bread and took a huge bite, chewing slowly, watching her. "You look like you've got the burdens of the world on your shoulders."

She poked her fork at the eggs. Yellow yoke spread over the plate. "I don't think we should get married."

"Yeah, you keep telling me that." He continued to eat as if nothing were wrong.

"And you keep moving ahead anyway. I mean it, Joshua. I will not marry you."

"What about our baby?"

She placed her hands over her stomach. Their baby. It hurt to even think about her. His dark hair, her blue eyes? Lauren's critical health problems. The very real chance she would lose her job and reputation if she didn't marry Joshua. She closed her eyes so she wouldn't have to meet his increasingly angry gaze. "You don't have to acknowledge her, but I'll let you see her whenever you want."

He slammed his fork down. "Well, that's just great. Everybody in six counties knows we've been seeing each other. Who are they going to think is the father when you start swelling up like an over-ripe watermelon?"

She turned an angry look on him. "Maybe I don't think we should compound a mistake by making a lifetime commitment neither of us wants!"

Unexpectedly his hand came up to cradle her

face. Ellie fought the urge to close her eyes and nestle into his caress by staring at the cold eggs congealing on her plate.

"Look at me and tell me you don't care, Ellie."

She hesitated, the words sticking in her throat like dry toast. "I don't." She scowled, staring at a point just above his ear.

The pad of his thumb glided over her lower lip, as if he wanted to erase her frown. "I think you're scared spitless, is all. You think our baby will be sick like Lauren's been and that I'll leave. Like your father did." His fingers caressed her neck, slid beneath the mass of her hair to cup the back of her head. "I swear I won't let you down."

"That's what my mother thought, too," she scoffed.

He dropped his hand away and gulped his coffee. "You don't know why he left."

"Well, neither do you, but it seems pretty obvious. He didn't really give a damn about his wife or his family. In ten years he's never sent a postcard or called to see if Lauren has even survived. I will never forgive him for that, and I won't give you a chance to do the same thing. I want you to leave." She removed the diamond heart necklace and carefully placed it in his hand. "I can't accept this."

He dropped the chain on the table. "I don't take gifts back." Pushing his chair away, he stood, then grabbed his Stetson from the peg on the wall. "The answers are right in front of you, but you've let yourself get too bitter to see them."

"What is that supposed to mean?"

"We'll discuss this after Lauren gets home from the hospital. You can call me at the ranch if you want to talk before then."

"Don't hold your breath."

He jammed his hat on. "This isn't over. Not by a long shot."

A few minutes later, he climbed in the Jaguar and roared down the driveway. Ellie rested her head in her hands and tried not to cry but the tears fell anyway, landing in the middle of her plate. Her stomach pitched under the emotional turmoil of the past few hours and the too strong coffee. She rose, scraped the plate into the disposal, then sank back down into her chair.

He deserved more than she could give him. An attentive wife, healthy children. Once he thought it through, he'd realize she was right. He'd visit the baby at first, then less and less. Maybe he'd help out financially for a while, but like most men, he'd lose interest as he got caught up in his own life again. He'd forget about the magic they'd shared.

She never would. The memory of being with him was burned into her and would remain forever.

Joshua arrived at Belle Ranch in a mood as black as a tar pit. He'd thought things were progressing pretty well. Lord knows he'd just about tied himself in knots trying to please Ellie, trying to make sure she knew he thought she was special. What a waste of time. So much for Barrett's advice.

But the truth was, he had enjoyed doing all those things for her. The little sparkle of surprise in her eyes made his heart lurch. Made the room suddenly seem devoid of oxygen.

He really was in it deep.

The mothers pretty much scattered as soon as he strode into the house. Except for Rosemary. Like a burr, she attached herself to him and followed him from the hall to the kitchen where he poured himself a mug of coffee, then into his study.

"Why isn't Ellie with you?"

"Problems with her little sister." He sat at the desk and busied himself with paperwork, hoping Rosemary would get the point and leave him alone with his dark thoughts. The documents from DJ emerged from beneath Barrett's ranch reports. Maybe if he could find Ellie's father . . . .

Rosemary frowned. "But then why aren't you there? She needs you."

"She doesn't seem to think so," he retorted, before he could stop himself. Hell, he'd never seen anyone so determined not to need anybody else. "She's so busy worrying about her sister, she's even trying to back out of the wedding."

"Oh dear." Rosemary sank back into her chair and was silent for several moments. "But then what will you do about the baby?"

Joshua choked on his coffee. "What?"

"Honestly, Joshua. Your mothers aren't as unobservant as you want to believe. You're thirty-five. Talk of marriage used to give you hives. So when you suddenly bring home a woman and announce she's your fiancée, naturally, I thought it was something like that, but the soda crackers and gingerale before breakfast were a dead giveaway."

"I had hoped no one noticed."

"We all did. Esther has us crocheting booties and working on a quilt. We decided the bedroom across from the master would make a lovely nursery."

"If you're assuming she's going to go through with the wedding you're making a pretty big assumption based on our conversation this morning. I don't really think I should have to drag her kicking and screaming down the aisle."

Rosemary shrugged. "Then tell her you love her."

He should have known better than to take another mouthful of coffee when she was sitting there making outrageous statements. "But I—" he sputtered.

She patted him on the arm as if he were still a green high school boy. "Ask yourself why you're feeling as if the world had stopped eating ice cream. Then tell me why you've been jumping through hoops if you don't love her. Because if that's the way you carry on when you merely like someone, I'm not sure I can imagine what more you could do."

Rosemary stood, went to the bookcase and took down the picture of his parents' wedding. "I know it's been difficult for you boys to understand why your father felt the need to get married so many times." She sighed. "He loved your mother very deeply, but I'm afraid I can't say the same about the rest of us. He was lonely, trying to fill the emptiness, and we all had something to give. I guess that's why the five of us are able to get along as well as we do. Each of us knows we never had his heart."

Joshua stared at her, touched by her admission. "Aw, come on, Rosemary. You know he cared about you."

"Of course. But some people love only once. He needed a mother for you and Barrett, and I fit the bill. I've never regretted it for a moment, even though it didn't last between us."

"He was very unhappy about the course you and Barrett had set for your lives, that's why he put the outlandish provision in his will. All he really wanted was for you to be happy."

"And Belle Ranch to stay in the family forevermore," he observed dryly.

"Naturally. But since you do too, how can you fault him for that?"

Good point. He didn't like being manipulated, that was all.

Like he'd been maneuvering Ellie from the night he'd met her? He wondered if she'd feel differently about marrying him if they didn't have the little coercion factor due in another six months. Would she have even agreed to keep seeing him?

She cared about him, he knew she did. It showed in the soft look she had in her eyes when she thought he wasn't watching. In the way she touched him. The way she'd come to him last night, warm, giving, and full of fire.

He speared his fingers through his hair and rested his elbows on the desk. If only he hadn't agreed to keep Danny Hirsch's secret. "Mom, what would you do if you learned something in confidence that had the potential to change someone's life? For the better, only you couldn't tell them because you'd promised someone else you wouldn't?"

Rosemary shook her head. "Sounds pretty confusing."

"I can't tell you what it is or who it's about. I'm just wishing I hadn't made a certain promise."

"But you did. Seems like the only thing to do is get that someone to release you from your promise. Or maybe have them do the telling."

That was it. He looked up. Rosemary's face was full of warmth and affection. All he had to do was to convince Danny to come clean with the Winfields, and Ellie would realize marrying Joshua was what she should do, what she wanted.

Wouldn't she?

The awful thought occurred to him that once Ellie knew there was no reason she shouldn't marry and have as many children as she wanted, she might realize she'd never had the opportunity to do any looking around. Thinking about her looking at another man made him feel a little crazy with anger, although he knew he was being unfair.

He'd had plenty of time to sow some oats. Ellie hadn't, and he liked it that way just fine, but he wanted her to come to him because he was the one she wanted, not because he was her only choice.

She cared about him, but she'd never uttered any words of love either. What if she didn't, or wouldn't admit it because he hadn't? Would she still agree to marry him? What about their child?

What a mess.

"Joshua?" Rosemary rested a hand on his shoulder. "If you know of a way to work things out with Ellie, then you owe it to yourself, to her, and to your baby to do it. You do love her, don't you?"

He placed his hand over hers and was silent for several minutes. Thoughts of Ellie danced through his mind. Her loving, giving nature. Her unselfish loyalty. The way he felt inside when she curled against him. "Yeah. I love her." Rosemary was right. He had to find a way.

No way was he giving up his own child. Or Ellie. He loved her too much to lose her.

Ellie stood at the window of Lauren's hospital room at the Cleveland Clinic and stared out at the gray drizzle. Jenna had gone back to the hotel to take a nap, leaving Ellie to keep Lauren distracted and amused until her little sister had fallen asleep, exhausted from the tests she'd undergone that morning.

Tomorrow would be the moment of truth. Lauren's surgery was scheduled for six a.m. In less than twenty-four hours, they would know if Lauren would be able to enjoy a full and normal life, or if she'd be condemned to medication and one surgery after another for the rest of her life.

She glanced at her watch. Four-thirty. Joshua would still be at the creamery. How she wished she could call him. The heart pendant rested beneath her shirt, the gold warm from her skin. It was silly to wear it now that things were over between them, but she couldn't seem to give up the little bit of comfort it offered.

He'd asked her to let him know about the surgery. It should be okay to call him just for that. Certainly he deserved that and wouldn't think it meant anything more. She picked up the phone beside Lauren's bed and dialed his mobile number.

The sound of his voice sent a flood of warmth and remembrances chasing through her. Then disappointment as she realized she'd reached his voice mail. Trying to keep her words crisp and businesslike, she left a message.

Joshua replayed the message for the tenth time, trying to get a handle on his hurt and anger. As if she had carefully scripted what she would say to him, Ellie sounded cold and distant.

Scared, lonely and unsure, he realized as he listened to the message again, then erased it.

She needed him, damn it. Whether she wanted to admit it or not, she could use someone to lean on right now. Although she and Jenna were close, Jenna was not cool in a crisis. He remembered her near hysteria the night Lauren had gotten sick. No wonder Ellie felt like she was carrying a double load.

Ellie needed him, and he was damned if he was going to sit around waiting for her to ask for his help.

Ellie gripped Jenna's hand tightly and watched the gurney carrying Lauren disappear through the double doors of the operating room. She squeezed her sister's hand. "The doctor said we can't expect to hear anything for at least an hour, probably longer. Come on, let's grab some breakfast, then you can help me with that afghan I'm trying to make."

Too tense and worried to eat much, Ellie picked the raisins out of a bowl of cold cereal and downed a glass of milk. Jenna didn't do much better, leaving most of her oatmeal untouched. Several times she seemed on the verge of saying something, then she'd sigh and continue stirring her oatmeal. Finally, they left the coffee shop and returned to the family waiting room to await word of Lauren's surgery.

In the corner a man sat, cradling a Styrofoam cup in his hands, cowboy hat pulled low. Ellie's heart lurched although she knew it wasn't Joshua. She missed him so much she ached all the way to her soul. If only . . . .

No way would he come all the way to Cleveland when she'd made it plain she didn't want him there. Which was just as well. Seeing him again would only weaken her resolve and make her question the decision she'd made the morning Lauren had been sick.

No, she had done the right thing by sending him on his way. He deserved far more than she could ever give him.

The man rose and started toward them, his slow gait increasingly familiar.

"Danny! What on earth are you doing here?" Ellie gave him a hug, then stepped back so Jenna could do the same.

He pushed his hat back and grinned warily. "Thought maybe you could use some company on the watch. Heard anything yet?"

Ellie shook her head and sat in one of the cushioned chairs arranged in small groupings. Jenna sat beside her and after a few awkward moments,

Danny pulled up a chair opposite.

"Who's taking care of the stock?" Ellie smoothed her skirt over her knees.

Danny rubbed his chin. "Hope you don't mind, but when a friend offered to keep an eye on both places, I just couldn't refuse the chance to be with my girls."

Touched, Ellie leaned forward and squeezed his arm. "That's sweet." Apparently another of their neighbors couldn't resist the opportunity to help when they knew she had no way to object. She wondered how Danny had managed to finance a high priced last minute plane ticket, but knew it wasn't her place to pry.

"Actually, I've got a double barreled reason to be here." Danny finished his coffee and set the cup on an end table. "I've got something to tell you that's not gonna be easy to say. Or to hear."

His words were directed to both of them, but his gaze fastened on Ellie. "I'm breaking a promise I made to your mama, Ellie. Maybe if I'd realized what was really going on I would have said something a long time ago, but I never knew just what your reasons were for being so determined to stay on the farm. Just as I didn't know why you called things off with Bellinghausen, since I know you've got a baby on the way."

Embarrassment heated her face as anger began to bubble in her blood. Joshua had a lot of nerve telling her neighbor anything about their private lives.

"Did he put you up to this?"

"No, ma'am. He didn't tell me you were pregnant, either. I figured that out, I just didn't know you were tying yourself in knots over it."

Ellie looked down at her clasped hands. "I don't know how I'll manage if my baby is as sick as Lauren's been."

Danny placed his hand over hers. "It won't happen."

Tears burned behind her eyes, but she refused to let them fall. "That's what Joshua keeps trying to tell me, but how can either of you know that? Lauren's condition is hereditary. The doctors are certain of that at least."

"I know, I know." Danny's voice was strangled. "That's what I'm trying to tell you, Ellie. You don't have to worry about your baby because you and Jenna have a different daddy than Lauren does."

Jenna gasped. Her lips trembled while tears brimmed in her eyes. "Danny Hirsch, how can you say such an outrageous thing?"

Ellie held his gaze, and he gripped her hands, refusing to let her pull away from him when the reality of what he was saying pounded into her mind and made her head ache.

Subtle similarities between her baby sister and the neighbor she'd known most of her life stared back at her, the reality of what he was trying to tell them gradually seeping in to shatter what she'd built her life on for the last ten years.

Oh, my God. How could her mother have done this to her and Jenna?

"I meant to take your mama's secret to my own grave, I promised Louise I would, but Joshua is right: thinking what you do is hurting you one helluva lot more than the truth will."

"Joshua knows?" Ellie's throat burned with indignation. How could he keep such a secret from her when he knew how frightened she was? How could Danny not have told her the truth ten years ago? That was even harder to accept than the knowledge of her mother's indiscretion.

"I didn't want you to hate me," he whispered as if he heard her thought. "And I couldn't bear to have you think ill of your beautiful mother."

How scared and alone her mother must have felt. And Danny, too. Mourning a woman when he couldn't admit to anyone he had loved her. Ellie's heart ached.

"Knows what?" Jenna's voice emerged in a horrified whisper.

"Joshua has known for a while, but I made him promise not to tell you. You see, Ellie, Jenna," he swallowed nervously. "I'm Lauren's father."

Chapter Sixteen

Ellie downed another cup of tea. Lauren had been in surgery for an hour and a half but it felt more like weeks. Danny continued to share an uneasy silence with her and Jenna. Although she longed for distance and a place to contemplate what he'd just told them, Ellie couldn't deny him the right to keep the vigil with them.

Danny's story made a lot of things that had troubled her over the years fall into place. Other people in Blanco had helped them at various times during the past ten years, but no one had given as much as Danny had. Somehow he'd just pitched in and gotten things done without giving her the chance to protest until she'd no longer felt the need to object.

She still worried about the difficulties her mother had giving birth to Lauren, but maybe Taylor was right and the problems were because of Mother's late-in-life pregnancy and were nothing for Ellie to be concerned about for herself.

If Joshua knew about her mother and Danny, that might explain why he'd been so insistent on getting married. No reason not to have more children to carry on the Bellinghausen name.

As much as the thought of carrying his child filled her with giddy elation, the reaffirmation that he only wanted to marry her because of the baby made her feel like a brood mare.

She loved him, but couldn't live with the idea of being nothing more than a means to an end for him.

As if from a long way off, Ellie heard her name being announced over the intercom. Jenna shook her by the shoulder. "Ellie, that's us. Lauren must be out of surgery."

Ellie hurried to answer the telephone set up in the waiting room. Dr Tobias was on the other end of the line.

"Miss Winfield. I'm pleased to be able to tell you that the surgery went very well. We were able to perform a repair instead of a replacement valve surgery. Your sister is going to be just fine."

Ellie sank into a chair, waves of relief washing over her. "Then she won't need any more surgery."

"This should be it. We'll talk more later, and you'll be able to see her in intensive care in a few hours."

Ellie hung up the phone and stood to hug Jenna. "She made it."

Danny stood awkwardly to one side, twisting his cowboy hat in his hands. One arm wrapped around her sister, Ellie extended her other hand to him.

"Come on, Danny. We might as well start acting like a family."

Gratitude and relief softening the lines etched by

hard work and worry on his face, he put an arm around each of them and hugged them hard before releasing them. "I am deeply sorry for what you've suffered the past years. You've got a good man in Bellinghausen, though, Ellie. He truly wanted to be here with you, but gave up his seat on the plane to me instead."

Jenna stood back and wiped her eyes with a tissue. "Guess this means you'll be married soon."

Ellie stooped to gather up her tote bag and purse, more to hide the hope she was sure showed in her eyes. Joshua deserved to marry for love. She couldn't let him settle for less. "I really don't think so."

Jenna sniffed. "Oh, Ellie don't be dense. The man is bananas over you, and the way you glow when you're near him, it hurts to look at you."

"But what about you? And Lauren."

"I'll miss you both terribly, but I'll understand if she wants to go with you to Belle Ranch. Think of the opportunities she'll have there."

"The farm," Ellie continued, not daring to make plans when she didn't see how she could resign herself to be Joshua's wife of convenience.

Jenna smiled. "I'm giving you Spotty as a wedding present. Heck, he should be yours anyway, you're the one who's all fired up to continue the breeding business. I'll bet you and Barrett will really make an even bigger success of Belle Ranch."

"But Jenna,–"

"Let's go stake out the ICU. Then once we know Lauren's out of the woods, we can grab a real breakfast." For the first time in their lives, Jenna seemed determined to take charge and led the way from the operating waiting room to the new area where Lauren had been moved.

"What will you do if I leave?" Ellie hurried to keep up with her sister's longer stride.

"I've got a couple of ideas." Jenna's eyes had a faraway look. "Just have to get them worked out."

Danny kept pace with Jenna's chatter. "Much as I hate to think of Lauren leaving Ellison's Farm, I think it's better if we don't rock the boat in Blanco. I can't let an old scandal hurt y'all. With your permission, Ellie, I can come visit her, and maybe in a couple of years you might want to tell her the truth about her father."

"Maybe she should know her father didn't abandon her."

Danny rested his hand on her arm. "Don't be too hard on your dad for that. He knew Lauren wasn't his and that's what he couldn't live with, not the fact that your mama was so sickly."

Maybe. But that didn't change the fact that he'd walked away from his two daughters and left her mother to die alone.

Seeing Lauren in intensive care was harder than Ellie would have imagined. The doctor said she was going to pull through okay, but the reality of seeing her chalky white and quiet, tubes running every which way, frightened Ellie more than she wanted to admit.

Jenna only lasted a couple of minutes before she excused herself and, looking pale and scared, made her way from the room.

"You and Joshua can get married now, Ellie." Lauren's voice was hoarse and raspy.

"Oh, Buttercup." Tears stinging her eyes, Ellie took Lauren's small hand in hers. She didn't have the strength to tell her little sister that there would be no wedding. How could Ellie expect Joshua to still want to marry her after what she'd said to him? Why should he have to when he didn't love her? Nearly overcome with dizziness, she gripped the side rail of Lauren's bed.

"Miss Winfield." The ICU nurse spoke her name again. "You have to leave now. You can see your sister later."

Somehow she made her way past the row of other patients, the door from the intensive care unit looking like it was a million miles away. The strain and lack of food combined to make her feel as if she were floating. She had to get out of here before she fainted, something that would undoubtedly frighten Lauren, even in her somewhat limited awareness.

Spots danced in front of her eyes, but she made it to the door, pushed on it and found the hall. Then her knees buckled, and she crumbled, pitching

forward and falling into strong arms and the familiar
scent of leather and sandalwood.

Joshua.

She started to cry. Throwing her arms around his
neck, she gave up the struggle and let him pick her
up as if she a child. "I need you," she mumbled,
tears spilling freely.

His chuckle rumbled reassuring against her
cheek. "About damn time you admit it. I love you,
Ellie Winfield and I promise I will never let you
down."

Two days later, Jenna and Danny had gone to the
cafeteria to eat, and Ellie and Joshua found
themselves alone for the first time. He loved her.
The thought filled her with awe. Scarcely daring to
believe it could be true, she sat next to him in
Lauren's semi-private room and watched her little
sister sleep.

She stole a glance at him and found him watching
her, an intent look on his face. She sighed. "I guess
you think we should set a date."

He pushed his cowboy hat back on his head.
"Nope."

No? Ellie felt the walls closing in on her. He'd
said he loved her. Why wouldn't he still want to get
married?

Glancing over at the sleeping child, he rubbed his
chin. "You know, it occurred to me that we went

from an improper beginning to an improper everything else. Including a world-class lackluster proposal." He eased from the chair and knelt before her, then removed his hat and placed it on the chair. "I couldn't understand why you were so unenthusiastic about getting married when I was certain you cared about me."

The look of uncertainty in his eyes stabbed her heart. She'd been wanting him to tell her he loved her, and she'd never said it to him. She cradled his face in her hands. "I do love you, Joshua," she whispered, then repeated it for good measure.

"Then we're on the right track at last." He fumbled in his shirt pocket, then took her left hand. She felt a return of exasperation. If he'd gone and bought her some flashy ring–He slid the ring on her finger. "I love you, Ellie. Will you marry me and let me be a proper father to our children?"

She stared down at the unusual ring, a large marquise cut stone of blue-green surrounded by a circle of round diamonds with baguette diamonds on the sides of the wide gold band. Her breath caught in her throat. "Oh, Joshua. I want to marry you, I just don't know."

He placed his finger against her lips. "I understand and I promise to stop pressuring you. When you feel comfortable about how Lauren's doing we'll get married. At the farm, like you wanted. Do you like the ring?"

"It's beautiful." She raised her gaze to his.

"It belonged to my mother. That was her birthstone, one you rarely see except in antique jewelry. If you'd rather have something else—"

His mother's ring. He'd given her something that must mean more to him than anything else he possessed.

Ellie threw her arms around his neck. "I love it. I love you. This means so much to me."

His lips found hers, kissing her with a tender passion unlike anything that had gone before as his hands feathered down her sides and settled at her waist. For the first time in her life, she felt as if the world were hers. Lauren was going to recover and would be able to lead a normal life. She no longer had to fear for her own child, or that she'd have the same problems delivering a baby as her mother had with Lauren. Jenna, bubbling with secret plans of her own, would be just fine at Ellison Farms.

Now all they had to do was wait until Lauren had recovered sufficiently to hold up to the excitement.

Several weeks passed. Although Joshua saw Ellie every weekend, the days dragged in between Sunday night and Friday afternoon when he left Belle Ranch to spend the weekend at the farm. They hadn't made love since the night of Lauren's mysterious illness. The ache to hold her nearly exceeded his fear that she would change her mind again about getting married.

No, he wouldn't rest easy until Ellie was beside him at night. Every night, at Belle Ranch.

Ellie called him at the creamery on Thursday afternoon. Anxiety about why she'd call him when she never did tempered the pleasure of hearing her voice.

"Everything okay?" His voice emerged sharper than he'd intended. Her hesitancy came over the line loud and clear. Aw, hell. Now what?

"Are you going to be at the farm this weekend?"

He pictured her in the roomy kitchen, wrapping the telephone cord around her hand, trying to find a way to tell him not to bother coming out. Or that Lauren had taken a turn for the worse. He steeled himself for bad news. "I was planning to."

"Good. It's supposed to be sunny. Maybe a little hot but I guess that's okay."

Anticipation coiled tight in his belly. He unclenched his hand and sat back in the chair. "Did you call to give me the weekend forecast, Ellie? Any chance of a hot sultry night?"

She laughed. "Actually I thought Saturday might be a good day to get married. If that's okay with you."

Okay? He wondered how he'd last two more days. "I'll bet I can round up the mommas and Barrett for a wedding."

"Good. Jenna and I will have everything ready here." Her voice dropped, became warm and inviting, sending a shiver through him.

"I love you, Joshua."

She hadn't told him since they'd been in Cleveland. He hadn't realized he'd been practically holding his breath, waiting to hear her say the words again. Love, relief, and satisfaction flowed through him. "I love you, too, Ellie. Are you sure we have to wait until Saturday?"

Two days. Forty-eight hours. How was he going to get through it?

Saturday afternoon Joshua stood beneath the centuries old live oak by the river that wound through the farm, and waited for Ellie and her sisters. Barrett, the mommas, Danny, Taylor, Ellie's co-worker, Mandy, and her husband were the only guests in attendance. The enormous tree formed a leafy cathedral and shaded them from the hot Texas sun, but not the humidity. He wiped a linen handkerchief across his forehead and resisted the urge to look at his watch.

"Think you'll stop sweating after she says I do?"

Barrett's good-natured gibe made Joshua scowl. He didn't want to admit, not even to his brother, the extent of his worries about Ellie changing her mind. Damn if she wasn't one unpredictable woman.

He glanced at their five stepmothers, each wearing a satisfied expression. "If only because now the mommas can focus all their match-making talents on you."

"Huh." Barrett's gaze fastened on Taylor, dressed in a simple pale blue dress, her prematurely gray hair shining in the sunshine. "Who's the babe with the silver hair?"

"Ellie's doctor. And she's too young, too sophisticated, and too intelligent for a farm boy like you."

Still staring at Taylor, Barrett grinned. "Is that a fact?"

Just then a flash of color caught Joshua's eye. Ellie, led by Lauren and Jenna, made her way from the house. Dressed in a pink lacy gown the color of the primroses covering the ground along the riverbank, carrying a bouquet of wild flowers, she looked like an angel. The wind caught at her blonde hair, loose except for a flowered clip holding it away from her face. His heart lurched. She was beautiful.

A few minutes later, he placed a gold band on her finger beside his mother's ring. She was his wife at last. He cradled her face in his hands and met her gaze. Ellie's eyes held all the love he'd been waiting for, and with a certainty that went all the way to his soul, he knew he'd found what he had been searching for all of his life.

How he loved her, and he didn't care who knew it or who heard him say it. He only wished he could shout loud enough for the whole world to hear. With his brother, the minister, and the rest of the family looking on, he said the words that a few months ago he never imagined he'd ever say.

"I love you, Ellie. With all my heart."

Her kiss told him she felt the same way.

Epilogue

Two weeks before Christmas, Ellie gripped Joshua's hand, trying to work through the pain that threatened to rip her in two.

Taylor's voice came from somewhere near Ellie's feet. "You're doing fine, Ellie. One more good push and we'll have her."

"Him," Joshua corrected automatically, wiping Ellie's brow and encouraging her.

In the intervening months since their marriage, he hadn't given up on his insistence that the baby would be a boy, although he'd steadfastly insisted they not be told the results of Ellie's sonograms. She hoped he wouldn't be let down.

"You're almost there, sugar."

A few minutes later, Ellie cried out and collapsed against the table. The sharp wail of a baby rent the air. She'd done it, without the anesthetics she'd feared had contributed to her mother's death.

"She's fine, Ellie. You are, too." Taylor's voice was strongly reassuring.

She? Ellie looked up into Joshua's eyes, praying she wouldn't find any trace of disappointment. His eyes shone suspiciously as he took the baby from

Taylor and lay their daughter on Ellie's bare stomach.

Ellie caught his hand and brought it to her cheek. How she loved him. "You're not disappointed?"

He reverently brushed his fingers over the baby's head and grinned. "Why would I be? She's all I ever wanted. Just like her mother."